AWKWARD INFIDELITY

AN AWKWARD NOVEL

RACHEL RHODES

Awkward in Print

Rachel Rhodes

First published 2019

Cover design by Canva

Edited by The Writer's Block

I never meant to have an affair. I certainly never meant to have one with my own husband, lying, cheating rat that he is. Aaron and I had been separated for almost a year when we bumped into one another at Starbucks. He was seeing Staci at the time – he had been since long before we split – and I'd been dating Blake for almost four months by then. Aaron had run into me. Literally. He'd knocked my Dirty Chai clear out of my hands, spilling it down the front of my new silk blouse. The blouse had been white before the steaming liquid turned it utterly sheer. Eyes fixed on my chest, Aaron had murmured, "you're looking good, Cat." Then he'd lifted those baby blues to fix me with his signature stare, and my stomach had done the conga. Five minutes later we were making out in the back-seat of a cab while the driver tried to watch us in the rear-view mirror. Another ten minutes, and we'd collapsed on the crumpled sheets of Aaron's unmade bed, which was still warm. I tried not to think about Staci and the longevity of her hatha yoga body heat.

"This was a mistake," I'd insisted as soon as it was over. Determinedly, I'd donned my still sodden blouse. Then we'd had sex again. Twice.

That was six weeks ago. Now, as I wait in my living room, watching the clock, I can recall every dirty, sexy second of it. The dial of the clock gives off a faint tick as it moves. It has just passed the half-hour mark when I hear a knock on my front door. Two short taps, followed by a pause. Another single tap. I'm opening the door before Aaron can finish the sequence, and I pull him inside by the front of his shirt.

"Easy!" he hisses as a button pops free of its thread and skitters across my hardwood floor. I know what he's thinking – that Staci might notice. Somehow it makes me want him more, rather than less. I throw a mental middle finger at Staci and groan against his lips. His breathing quickens. I know exactly what he likes, and how he likes it. We were together for five years and married for just short of two of those. Three weeks and two days short, if we're counting. I'd spent my second wedding anniversary trying to find myself in the bottom of a bottle of Tequila. All I'd found was the worm. No doubt Aaron had spent the evening plugged into Staci.

I never thought my marriage would end. Nobody does, I suppose, when they're walking down the aisle in that ironically white dress, with baby's breath twined through their hair. Aaron and I met in college, the University of California, Berkeley, during that time in a man's life when he's at his most uninhibited and open to experimentation. We'd been in the same drinking club at UCB. My single, stir-crazy mother, Viola, had raised me in a liberal household and encouraged me to embrace my sexuality. She claimed orgasms were my God-given right. My mother behaves like a bona fide hippy, though she's not yet forty-five. Still, I'd taken her lessons to heart and met Aaron's challenges head-on. The sex had been glorious and, at times, borderline depraved. I know all of Aaron's dirty little secrets, and believe me, some are so dirty that I doubt tree-hugging, yoga-teaching Staci would hang around if she knew half of them.

He's still bothered by the button. I can tell by the set of his jaw, the annoyance flashing in his ice-blue eyes. I twist in his arms and press my backside up against his groin, gyrating slightly. Distracted, his annoyance fades as his strong hands grip my hips, and I smile to myself as he hauls me into the bedroom, all thoughts of Staci blown right out of his mind.

"AM I SEEING YOU ON FRIDAY?" Aaron asks as he buttons up his shirt. It's always like this – the second we're done, he's up and out of the door as quickly as possible. I don't mind. We've never been great conversationalists. He pauses at the missing button. A small frown creases his brow. I bite my lip, knowing my answer isn't going to help his fast-deteriorating mood.

"Actually, I'm meeting Blake on Friday morning. We're having breakfast at *Verdure*." I may be showing off, just a little. *Verdure* is an exclusive new bistro uptown, where you pay a small fortune for a tiny portion of food to be prepared by some of the best chefs in the city. Blake is a surgical resident. He works long hours, but this Friday he has one of his rare days off. Conversely, Staci teaches three back-to-back yoga classes every Friday morning at the community center, which leaves Aaron with way too much free time on his hands. Aaron is a trust-fund baby. Technically, he runs one of his father's subsidiaries, but in reality, I've never known him to work a day in his life.

"Oh." He manages to convey an entire lifetime of disappointment into that one little word. I wish I didn't care.

"I can't cancel, he's already booked. And it's not as if *this*," I wave my hand between us, "is going anywhere."

I try to hide it, but he hears my longing, and his lips twitch upward in smug satisfaction. If I know all of Aaron's secrets, he knows all of mine. He can read me like an open book, and right now he knows that I want him to reconsider the separation. It's no big secret. I've wanted that since the day we split. He crooks his finger at me, and my and I forget how to breathe. *Play it cool, Cat.* My feet ignore my silent plea and slide forward of their own accord until I'm standing right before him. Exactly where he wants me. Aaron runs a long, lean finger down the hollow of my throat.

"Baby, you know I can't leave Staci. You and I, we've got something special, but we don't work the usual way. We've proved it."

"And yet we're not divorced yet," I snap, annoyed by all the '*we*' references when the real reason we didn't work had nothing to do with me and everything to do with him screwing Staci in our marital bed. Aaron's fingers dip under the lace of my bra, and my thoughts scatter.

"You want me to divorce you, Kitty Cat?" he murmurs.

I shake my head, no, as his fingers close around my nipple and squeeze hard enough to hurt.

"I didn't think so." His voice is hoarser now. With expert fingers, he reaches behind me and unhooks my bra. "Well, I guess if I'm not seeing you on Friday, we better make up for it now." I open my mouth to argue that I have work to do, but he's already plunging his hands into my hair and yanking back my head to claim my mouth.

I'm bow-legged by the time Aaron leaves, wishing, as I do every time we part, that he didn't have this hold over me. He's an asshole, but the sex is out of this world. Even better now that it's taboo. There's nothing quite as intoxicating as the risk of getting caught.

When I found out about Aaron's affair with Staci, I was devastated. Kicked in the gut, didn't leave the house for a week, drenched my pillow every night, shattered. There was nothing remarkable about that day, barring the fact that it turned out to be the day my life was turned upside down. It was just an average Monday. I was supposed to be meeting a potential new client, but he'd canceled at the last minute, and it was late enough in the day that I could play hooky, guilt-free. I'd stopped at the deli to get a few of the little pastries Aaron adored, grabbed two bottles of wine to go with them, and headed home, already thinking of new ways to greet him at the door, most of which involved lacy underwear, some of which involved no underwear at all.

I didn't even notice them at first. Thinking back, it's almost laughable how they lay, frozen, on the couch while I'd uncorked the wine and poured myself a glass, taken a long and leisurely sip, and contemplated whether I should call Aaron and let him know I was home early. I'd swilled the wine in my mouth, turned toward the living room, and sprayed it all over the counter. Staci had cowered beneath Aaron while I threw first the bottle and then half a dozen cream-filled pastries at his head.

I'm still not sure if it was my heart or my pride that was most shattered. I'd kicked him out, obviously. It was my name on the lease, and there was no way I was having Staci move into the apartment that I'd spent two years decorating. I'd paint-techniqued the hall myself, with a tiny paintbrush that covered about an inch an hour.

I hadn't seen Aaron for months after that. Secretly, I had hoped he would come crawling back, begging for forgiveness and oozing remorse. In reality, he had moved into a new apartment with Staci less than a month after our split. It had taken me a lot longer to move on. Despite my mother's increasing insistence that I should find myself a new lover, I'd found Aaron harder to shake than the herbs she brewed into her tea. It was, in fact, those herbs that finally got me out of my funk. A few months after the split, I'd gone over to spend an evening with my mother and ended up in the hospital. God knows what she put in that tea, but I was tripping out of my mind when I stumbled into the E.R, one arm draped around her slim shoulders, the other holding a half-eaten hamburger, which I'd refused to relinquish even after I'd started throwing up.

Blake had been on duty. He'd taken one look at me, asked a few questions of my mother, who'd pretended not to be able to speak a word of English, and set up a drip. Two hours later, my mother, who'd recovered her command of the English language well enough to chat up the sister on duty, pushed off to a party and I'd sobered enough for a tidal wave of humiliation to wash over me.

"Your mom's quite something," Blake had said as he removed the drip.

"She's a little wild," I'd admitted. "And she's not Italian, obviously."

"If she were, I'd be worried, seeing as how she was speaking Spanish," he pointed out. "So, your mother is wild. What about you? Do you do this kind of thing often?"

"Do what kind of thing?" I asked, innocently. My mother had taught me well. To my amazement, his face had creased into a smile, and it was glorious. Like watching stone come to life.

"I'm not going to report you, Catrina," he'd said. I'd known a moment of passionate relief before I'd vomited all over his shoes.

"It's Cat," I'd told him before I left. "No one calls me Catrina anymore."

He'd looked at me with an unreadable expression on his face and said, "That's a pity. It's a beautiful name." I'd watched his broad back until it disappeared behind another curtain and found myself hoping the woman on the other side of it wasn't remotely attractive.

I'D CALLED my mom as soon as I got home. Judging by the screaming chaos in the background, the party was still in full swing. For the first few minutes, all she was interested in was whether Nurse Janine's shift had ended yet, and if so, did she mention if she was coming to the party. I answered honestly that I had no idea.

"I bet you fifty bucks that boy calls you," she'd slurred, then. I'd told her she was high. She may well have been, but as it turned out, she was also right.

For a long time, I didn't mention my budding relationship with Blake to any of mine and Aaron's mutual friends. My biggest fear was that he would use it as grounds to finally go through with divorce proceedings which, despite my growing feelings for Blake, wasn't something I was ready to accept. As it turns out, what actually happened was the complete opposite. Not a week after letting it slip, I'd bumped into Aaron at Starbucks. Or rather, he'd bumped into me. The rest, you already know. In rare moments of insanity, I find myself wondering if he'd masterminded the whole thing because he'd realized he might lose *me*. In reality, I know that Aaron simply doesn't like to lose.

I don't take a shower, preferring to keep the scent of him on me for as long as I can. I'm not seeing Blake until much later, so there'll be plenty of time to wash away the guilt. I grab an apple out of the fruit bowl on the counter, shove my laptop in my bag, and head for the coffee shop down the street, which serves as my informal office. I'd studied commerce in college and been smart enough to capitalize on the rise of e-commerce. I now run online stores for a healthy portfolio of customers, including two rapidly emerging brands, and I take a hefty cut of their proceeds in return.

Amy, the regular morning waitress, greets me with a smile. "You want the usual, Cat?"

"Make it a double, please. I have a ton of admin to get through today."

"Coming right up."

I work right through lunch, with Amy refilling my coffee cup every hour. By the time my laptop battery runs low, I've done as much as I can for today.

"You want anything to eat?" Amy asks as she passes by on her way to check on another table. The patron is a slightly creepy-looking man in his early thirties with a mop of blond hair and a fleshy lower lip, who's been casting surreptitious glances my way all morning.

"No, I'm good," I tell Amy. "Just the bill, please."

I leave Amy a generous tip and head home. When the elevator opens on my floor, I'm horrified to find Blake at my door. He's holding a huge bunch of lilies – my favorite, despite the negative connotation – and an unidentifiable DVD. Blake is old-school. He still hires movies the old-fashioned way, even though I have Netflix and unlimited streaming. I'm suddenly acutely aware that my body is coated in all things Aaron.

"What are you doing here?" I ask, mustering a smile. "I thought you were only getting off later tonight."

Blake's eyes crinkle at the corners when he smiles. "It turns out I forgot to log a few shifts. I've exceeded the maximum limit, so they sent me home. Can't have us falling asleep with a scalpel in our hands." He leans in to kiss my cheek, and I duck my head, terrified to get too close.

"Sorry, I reek. I didn't bother showering after gym this morning." The lie rolls easily off my tongue as I quickly unlock my door and step inside. "Make yourself comfortable, I'm going to hop in the shower, and then we can catch up." He gives me a curious look but doesn't argue.

The water is scalding. As it runs over me, I scrub my skin until it's red and angry. God, I am such a bitch. I vow for what must be the twentieth time that I'm going to end things with Aaron. Blake is a good guy – far too good for me if the truth be told. Why the hell am I risking what we have for a man who self-admittedly has no intention of reconciling? *Because he gets you,* the devil on my left shoulder whispers in my ear. *Because you like things a little rough, a little dangerous, and Blake* is *a good guy, but you want a bad one.*

Hair still wet from the shower, I pull on a pair of leggings and an oversized shirt.

"You smell good," Blake murmurs as I cozy up beside him on the couch. He smells of antiseptic and aftershave. It's a wholesome and heady combination. This time when he leans in for a kiss, I turn my face toward him. My stomach disappears. I am most definitely attracted to Blake. He's smart and his sense of humor is just quirky enough to be original. He also overthinks almost everything. I never know what's going on behind those hazel eyes. Hell, in another year he'll be a fully-qualified general surgeon. At least a head taller than Aaron, and twice as broad in the shoulders, I can only imagine how his female patients must fawn over him. I must be crazy.

"How long do I have the pleasure of your company, before your pager interrupts us?" I tease.

"I'm only back after the weekend, so we have four whole days to ourselves. Speaking of which," he says, withdrawing his pager and dropping it into the drawer of the low coffee table.

"Wow, you really are off duty," I say.

He kicks the drawer closed with his foot. "Silence is golden."

"What did you get?" I ask, gesturing at the DVD on the table.

He laughs, a rumble that starts deep in his chest. "*Wedding Crashers*."

I can't help but grin. Blake has a deep and abiding love for Vince Vaughn. I lean forward and kiss him again, letting my mouth linger on his.

"You get it set up, I'll make the popcorn."

"You don't want me to order anything in?" he asks, as my stomach gives a low rumble.

"No, popcorn will be fine. Unless you're hungry?"

He shakes his head. "I grabbed a sandwich at the canteen before I left."

Snuggled up beside Blake on the couch, my feet wedged between his thighs for warmth, my head on his shoulder, it's so easy to forget Aaron. So easy to see a life with Blake – a future filled with marriage, and babies, mortgages and seaside vacations. He's the man for whom your mother would sell her soul to the devil, to see you end up with. Aaron, on the other hand, is the devil who'd claim it.

I'm so lost in thought that I barely pay attention to the movie, until I feel Blake's shoulder shaking under my cheek.

"What is it with you and Vince Vaughn?" I tease, as he lets out another rumble of laughter.

"Oh, come on! He's hilarious. Look at him!" he points at the screen. Admittedly, the sight of Vince trying to blow off Isla Fisher in the bathroom, while she climbs all over him like a rabid monkey, is pretty hysterical.

"We look a bit like them," Blake says, between bursts of laughter. Vince is tall, like Blake, and my hair is long, and red, like Isla's, but other than that, I don't see a resemblance.

"You're better looking," I say. Blake gives me a heart-stopping smile and kisses my hand.

After the movie, he leads me by the hand to my bedroom.

"You must have been in a rush this morning," he says at the doorway. "You didn't even make your bed."

I cringe at the sight of the rumpled sheets, even while my eyes scan the room, searching for any evidence of Aaron. Blake takes a step toward the bed, but I grab his arm, pulling him back.

"Come here," I murmur, backing up until my back hits the cold brick of the hall. Blake smiles, uncertain, so I pull him against me and kiss him deeply. I don't want to make love to him in that bed. He doesn't deserve that.

"What are you doing?" he mumbles as I pull his shirt up and over his head.

"Rewarding you for all those extra shifts you worked," I say, and then I silence him with another kiss.

I watch the suds build up against the washer door with grim satisfaction as all trace of Aaron is washed away. After we'd made love, I'd run Blake a bath and used the opportunity to change the sheets, which assuaged some of my guilt. The next four days will be the longest stretch of time Blake and I have spent together uninterrupted and, to my surprise, I'm looking forward to it.

"Laundry?" Blake asks when he tracks me down. He's wearing only a pair of tracksuit pants, and a towel around his neck. "At this time of night?"

"I spilled my wine," I say, waving the half-full, just poured glass toward him.

I WAKE up early on Thursday to get some work done while he sleeps in. I ignore three texts from Aaron, which had come in late last night, put my phone on silent, and climb back into bed.

The texts start up again that afternoon, detailing every single thing Aaron would do to me the next time we met. With each one, opened in private and deleted as soon as I've read it, my stomach curls in a heady mix of loathing and longing. I don't reply, and the texts become increasingly desperate. I know how Aaron thinks. By ignoring him, I am fanning the flames of his desire. This is a game that I know how to play, and the longer it continues, the more the tension builds. Still, I pay special attention to Blake. I care deeply for him, and what he doesn't know won't hurt him. It's not as if I actually plan to meet Aaron, at least not until Blake is back at work. This is Aaron's punishment for how he's treated me. If it goes on long enough, Aaron might even come to his senses and leave Staci for good. At least, that's what I tell myself as I try to ignore the squirming desire in the pit of my stomach.

Later that night I'm reading in bed when the next text comes through. Horrified, I check to make sure that Blake is asleep before I read it. This one is completely different to the rest. Gone is the flirtatious playfulness, and the coarse language.

I need to see you.

Hastily, I type a response. *I'm busy. We can talk next week.*

I hit send. A moment later another text comes through,

This can't wait.

Blake shifts in his sleep.

It'll have to.

He's already typing, but I switch my phone off and toss it on the nightstand. I snuggle closer to Blake and slip my feet between his legs to warm them, but I register nothing of the pages I read after that.

"I hope you're hungry," Blake teases the following morning as we set out for Verdure. I'd offered to make breakfast for him at home, but he'd insisted we keep our booking.

"I'm starving," I laugh. My hand is dwarfed in his, my palm tingling where our skin touches. We take a cab and are seated by 9.05.

"I need a coffee, the biggest you can rustle up," I tell the smiling waiter.

"Make it two," Blake adds, just as the soft ping of a text sounds from my phone. I pull it from my purse and frown at the screen.

"Everything okay?" Blake asks, his brow furrowed in concern.

"Fine," I reply lightly. I slip the phone back into my purse. "Can you get me the three-cheese omelet? I'm just going to the ladies."

"Sure." He gets to his feet as I stand. I smile at the chivalrous gesture, but my heart is hammering. Aaron's text was only two words. *Bathroom, now.*

I slip into the ladies' room and quickly scan the stalls. They're all empty. For want of something else to do, I wash my hands and splash water onto my face. When I look up into the mirror, Aaron is right behind me.

I barely have time to react when his hands are up my skirt. My conscience screams no, but nothing comes out of my mouth except a startled gasp as Aaron snaps the elastic of my panties clean in two. At the sound, my breath hitches and some primal part of my brain roars to life, driving all reason from my mind. Aaron is already hard, and he flips me around to face him, lifting me off the floor so my thighs are straddling his waist. He carries me to the door and presses me up against it, a barricade for anyone who might try to open it from the outside. His teeth clash against mine as his tongue sweeps into my mouth. He doesn't say a word, but his eyes are furious, glittering with malice and desire. His hands leave my hips, but I clamp my legs more tightly around his waist, keeping myself aloft as he fumbles with his zipper. A guttural moan in my ear is the only warning before he's inside me. His hands squeeze my buttocks, and his lips move to my ear.

"Don't-ever-ignore-me-again." He punctuates each word with a thrust of his hips, and I bite my lip to keep from crying out at the intensity of it.

It's over in a matter of seconds. I collapse against his chest as the dam inside of me bursts, sending spasms through my entire body. Aaron releases his hold, ever so slightly, and lowers me to the floor. His eyes are flint, his lips smeared with my pale rose lip gloss.

I straighten my dress as he pulls up his pants. My panties are bunched tightly in his fist.

"I'm keeping these," he says, shoving them into his pocket. I shrug, not caring in the slightest. As the adrenalin leaves my body, reality is slowly reasserting itself. Blake, waiting just outside. All the progress I've made, gone in an instant. Aaron is never going to come to heel if he keeps getting what he wants so easily.

"You should go." I raise my chin and wipe at my own bruised lips. "This was a mistake."

The smile that spreads across his face is pure malevolence. "So you keep saying, Kitty Cat."

"Yeah well, one of these days I'm going to mean it." I don't wait for him to reply. Instead, I fling open the door, so quickly that he has to hurl himself behind it to avoid being seen by nearby patrons, and stalk back to my table.

"Everything okay?" Blake asks, his eyes searching mine.

"I'm fine, just feeling a bit flushed," I reassure him. Out of the corner of my eye, I see Aaron slip out of the ladies. He has the gall to blow me a kiss.

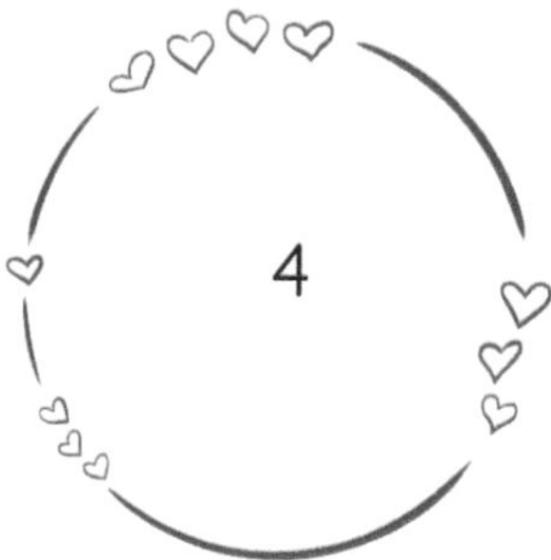

4

This time, I'm determined to stick to my guns. The high of being with Aaron fades fast, throwing me into a pit of despair and self-loathing. It's the twisted cycle of our toxic relationship. Blake goes back to work on Monday, and I settle into my familiar routine. A week passes, and then another, and I ignore every message Aaron sends me. I send his calls to voicemail and delete them without listening. I make sure to be out of the house first thing in the morning so he'll find an empty apartment if he tries to visit. Surprisingly, my relationship with Blake is improving by the day. Without the distraction of my affair with Aaron, I find it easier to focus on what's right in front of me. In week three, I offer him a key to my apartment, which is the ultimate gesture of commitment, given that its where most of my secret trysts with Aaron take place. Blake is genuinely delighted.

"DON'T FORGET I'm meeting the girls tonight," I tell him one Wednesday morning. We're in bed, snuggling before Blake has to report to the hospital for his shift. Given how close my apartment is to the hospital, he's spending most evenings here, and he's promised to wait up for me. "There's a few frozen pizzas in the freezer, or I could order something for you before I go?"

His arm tightens around my shoulders. "I'm perfectly capable of feeding myself, Cat. You go and enjoy yourself."

Since Aaron and I separated, I spend one evening a month with my two remaining girlfriends. Once, we'd been a huge group, but after the separation, most of our couple friends had chosen Team Aaron. Only Gwen and Bianca have kept in contact with me, but they're by far the best of the lot.

I arrive first and order a bottle of red wine for the table. Then there's the rigmarole of smelling it, swirling it around in the glass, and taking an appreciative sip, all of which is just for show because I wouldn't have a clue. I've only just picked up the menu to browse when Gwen arrives, her coat flapping behind her.

"I'm sorry I'm late, traffic was awful!" she announces at the top of her voice, oblivious of the fact that she's drawn the attention of the entire restaurant. Even if she didn't speak at the decibel level of a small choir, she would have it anyway. A leggy blonde, with chiseled cheekbones and a mega-watt smile, Gwen is one of the nicest people I know. A complete klutz, she's as likely to trip over her own feet as she is to forget her mother-in-law's birthday – which she has, four years straight – but people forgive her because she's too nice not to forgive. Bianca, short, dark, and furious, is the polar opposite of Gwen in every way possible. She arrives only a few minutes later, stalking through the restaurant as if the patrons seated at the tables between her and us exist for no other reason than to inconvenience her.

"Have you heard from Aaron?" Gwen asks. It's her standard opening question. I think that secretly Gwen still harbors hope that Aaron and I will reconcile and bring our circle back together. Gwen's husband, Jason, is one of Aaron's closest friends, and I know that she feels helplessly torn between her loyalty to me, and the pressure Jason puts on her to play nice with Staci.

"No." I give her my standard answer. Gwen and Bianca may be

my best friends, but even they would draw the line at what I've been up to with Aaron.

"I heard he's having trouble with Staci," Bianca announces, throwing her jacket over the back of her chair and slapping an elderly woman at the next table in the face with one sleeve.

I almost drop my glass. "What do you mean, having trouble?"

"She accused him of cheating on her, apparently," Bianca says, oblivious to the dark looks being cast her way by the woman's dinner companion. "Mike says Aaron was pretty pissed about the whole thing, but I told him once a cheater, always a cheater." Mike is Bianca's long-term boyfriend, whom she refuses to marry, despite him having asked at least three times.

Gwen nods in grave agreement and fills her glass. "I heard that too." She doesn't want to say where she heard it, and I don't probe. Neither of us likes to acknowledge that she sees Staci socially.

"Did she have any proof?" I ask carefully, trying to act nonchalant.

"Nothing she can pin down. She claimed she smelled another woman's perfume on his clothes, said it couldn't be hers because she doesn't wear perfume. It's toxic for your skin, apparently."

Bianca grimaces. "I've never understood what he sees in her."

"She's attractive," I offer graciously, while the devil on my left shoulder dances with glee at the thought that Aaron and Staci might be on the outs. There's no point in feeling guilty that I'm the reason – she's the one who had the affair with a married man.

Gwen shrugs. "You're prettier," she says.

"It's true," Bianca adds as I shake my head in mock-humility. I know I am. I was blessed with good genes, although I'm not sure whose. "Anyway, Aaron denied it and last he told Mike, the whole thing seemed to have blown over."

"Oh." I deflate faster than a balloon in a needlestack.

"Enough about Aaron," Gwen moans, taking a massive slug of champagne. "How is that gorgeous man you've been seeing?"

"Blake? He's fine. I gave him a key to my apartment," I confide.

"About time," Bianca sighs. "Why don't you just divorce Aaron and marry the sexy doctor, Cat? God knows you deserve it after what Aaron put you through."

I shake my head so vigorously my hair whips into my eyes. "Hell no. I'm never getting married again."

"Why not? Just because it didn't work out for you the first time doesn't mean you have to give up on the whole idea." Irony isn't Bianca's strong suit.

"You know this whole conversation is pointless, while she's still legally married, right?" Gwen points out. "Why *haven't* you divorced Aaron, anyway?"

I shrug. "I don't know."

"You should do it. It's time to move on with your life, Cat." This time, it's Bianca who nods in solemn agreement.

I raise my glass. Swirl the contents. "Maybe you're right," I concede, and then I chug back the entire glass.

IT TAKES me forever to fit my key into the lock, and when I finally do, I fall inside my apartment. A pair of strong arms catch me before I hit the floor.

"Easy there!" Blake croons, propping me up with an arm around my waist. I squint up at him in the dim light coming from the hall.

"You're beautiful," I say, placing my hand against his cheek.

He grins. "And you're drunk."

"We had wine. At dinner. In fact, I think I had wine *for* dinner," I add, frowning as I try to recall if I ate any of my ravioli.

"Then you need water, and fried eggs."

"That your professional opinion, Doctor Stanton?"

"Nope. Just years of college experience."

He leaves me on the couch with two Alka-Seltzer and a massive glass of water. I doze on and off to the sounds of him cooking in the kitchen, and then he rouses me gently and sets a tray on my lap. Eggs never looked so unappealing, but I try to eat a little, just to appease him. Unfortunately, I manage only two bites before I have to rush to the bathroom. When I emerge, I'm mortified. I've brushed my teeth twice, but I can still taste vomit.

"Sorry," I mumble. Blake leads me to the bed and tucks me in before climbing in beside me. "Believe me, I've seen worse. It goes with the territory."

"If we ever got married, I'd be Doctor Stanton," I say brightly.

Blake laughs, the low, familiar rumble against my ear. "I think you mean *Mrs.* Stanton," he teases, "but I'll take it."

The following morning, I wake up to an empty bed. There's a note on the pillow, along with two pills. I recognize Blake's untidy scrawl. *Had to go in early. Take these and sleep it off.*

I swallow down the pills with half a glass of water. Dry-mouthed and head-pounding, I totter into the bathroom to take a cold shower. Slowly the icy blast clears my head. I think about what Gwen and Bianca said last night, and for the first time, the idea of divorcing Aaron doesn't send a wave of panic through me. Aaron wasn't a great husband. In fact, he was a pathological liar and cheat, but for some reason, I've never been able to shake the hold he has over me. The sex is fantastic, obviously, but when you get down to the core, there's not much else. When I check my phone after breakfast, I have two X-rated texts from him, which only prove my point. Aaron only wants me because he can't have me. I can't keep fooling myself that his sudden yearning for me has nothing to do with my growing relationship with Blake. The proof is in the pudding. Every time my relationship with Blake kicks up a notch, Aaron's attention to me rises accordingly. Blake, on the other hand, wants all of me – the good, the bad, and the ugly. And, even if he's not 'the one', deep down, I know I'll never be truly happy with Aaron. Not now. Not anymore. Hell, I wasn't even that happy before Staci-Gate blew up in my face.

Feeling only marginally more human, I dress in a pair of blue jeans and a white jersey top which leaves one shoulder bare. I take a cab across town to the art gallery where my mom occasionally has paintings on display – when she bothers to paint any. It's a small but upmarket gallery, with stark white walls to offset the vibrant art it favors. The owner knows me well, and she greets me warmly as I step inside.

"Cat! How's my favorite customer?"

"Hey, Trish." I return her hug. "I'm good, thanks."

She gives me a wry smile. "I should've known you'd be in today." She ushers me to the back of the gallery, to where a small oil painting hangs under a white light. "I only hung it this morning. Although, how you always seem to know is beyond me."

"It's a gift," I say, enigmatically, and then walk past her to the far wall.

I recognize my mother's style immediately. Worse, I recognize the face of the nude woman she's painted – it's Janine, the nurse who was on duty the night I met Blake, and who I've met on more than one occasion since. My mother's flirting that night must have paid off after all.

"Gorgeous, isn't it?" Trish murmurs reverently as she comes to stand behind me. Gorgeous isn't the word I would use to describe the painting. Janine's ample flesh is on full-color display, her wrists and ankles bound in a chain mail of dirty needles. I'd recognize the grubby day bed she's spread-eagled over anywhere – it's adorned my mother's studio since before I can remember.

"I knew you'd love it," Trish continues, oblivious. "Every time a new Viola Davis comes in, I think of you. How many of hers do you own now? It must be at least a dozen."

"Twenty-seven," I reply automatically. I can almost hear her brain ticking, trying to work out which other gallery might be her competition. I could tell her, but I won't. My eye falls to the orange sticker. $2600. That's almost three hundred dollars more than the last one. Trish is pushing her luck, but I smother my sigh. "I'll take it."

She gives a delighted tinkle of laughter and claps her hands together. "Wonderful. Let me wrap it for you. Would you like me to have it delivered?"

"No need," I say, pulling out my card. "I'll take it now. And please make sure to mark me down as an anonymous buyer."

She arches her brow but doesn't comment as she lifts the painting down. I think she's let the topic go, but she tries one last time as she rings it up. "I do wish you'd let me tell Viola who you are. She pops in all the time, I'm sure she'd love to meet such a fan of her work."

"Anonymous," I insist, more firmly. Trish lowers her eyes first.

IT TAKES me less than a minute to find a cab. I dump the painting unceremoniously on the seat beside me and rue the fact that I just spent $2600 on yet another of my mother's paintings.

It had all started three years ago. Aaron and I were busy making wedding plans, and my mother, in a rare moment of responsibility, had decided to start painting again. Viola had gone to art school. She'd left before graduating, to have me, having been knocked up by one of her professors. She wouldn't ever tell me his name and, given that he'd known about me and chosen to pretend I didn't exist, I hadn't ever bothered to try to find him.

"You're getting married, Cat," my mom had announced during the one and only dress fitting she'd accompanied me to. "I have to learn how to support myself."

It had been a relief to hear her admit it. I didn't mind helping her out, but when I saw my hard-earned money being blown on booze and recreational drugs, it stung.

I'd supported her decision fully, and I'd even canceled an appointment with my wedding planner to accompany her to a local gallery which we thought might consider showcasing her work.

Unfortunately, the gallery decided that her flamboyant style wasn't quite the right fit for an exhibition. But they were prepared to display one of her paintings, which turned out to be a good thing as my mother, due to a combination of crippling self-doubt and a short-lived relationship with a man she'd met at the dress-fitting, hadn't bothered to paint any others. The painting, a small watercolor which was as abstract as it was intense, was hung the day before my wedding. Aaron and I honeymooned in Thailand, and I gave it little thought during the two weeks we were away. Only once we'd returned, floating back to earth after fourteen blissful nights away, did I learn that the painting had garnered absolutely no interest and my mother had fallen into a pit of drug-fuelled despair.

"It's only been two weeks," I'd told her when she'd sobered up enough to listen. "You have to give it time." She'd told me that hope was indeed a fickle mistress, and then disappeared to the bathroom, where she'd smoked a joint the size of a bratwurst. I'd found her hanging out of the bathroom window singing Chaka Khan while a group of pedestrians gathered on the street below, pleading with her not to jump.

The following morning, I'd marched into the gallery and bought the painting, insisting I be listed as an anonymous buyer. Sadly, no good deed goes unpunished. My mother's gloomy despair was replaced by a fireball of optimism fuelled by a manic desire to sell another painting. When it didn't sell, she slipped back into the dark place I hated. And so began a vicious circle. She would paint, and I would purchase. I'd never told Aaron. I didn't want him to know, didn't want to give him any ammunition to use against her. Aaron was never outright rude about my mother, but I could tell he thought of her as a bit of a joke, and it hurt more than I cared to admit. When she started 'selling' he'd given her a new, albeit begrudging respect, and I didn't want to take that away. My mother's chronic laziness was my saving grace. If she'd painted more frequently, I would probably have gone broke trying to sustain her constant need for validation.

"Miss?" the cab driver's voice brings me back to the present. "This is your stop, yes?"

I blink out of the window at my familiar apartment block.

"Yes, this is it. Thanks." I hand him a crumpled bill and hoist the painting out with me. Safely back inside my apartment, I stash it in the loft, along with twenty-seven others, and then I head back out to meet my mother for lunch.

"DARLING!" she calls as I weave through the busy bistro. She's wearing a floral kaftan, and there's a smudge of burnt orange paint on her cheek, but her eyes are bright and clear, and I breathe a sigh of relief that she's sober.

"You've been working," I say, giving her a brief hug before we take our seats.

"I woke up at five this morning and couldn't get back to sleep. I decided to make the most of it."

The waitress arrives with our menus, but my mom waves them away.

"A black coffee and a cappuccino, with almond milk, if you have," she says. "And bring us two garden salads. No cheese."

"I'll have cheese," I correct, "and regular milk, please." My mother arches her brow, but I ignore her. Despite her frequent attempts to convert me, I refuse to follow her vegan lifestyle.

"Just be grateful I'm not ordering a steak," I say. The waitress hides a smile.

"It's so barbaric," my mother sniffs. "I bet if you visited an abattoir, you'd quickly change your tune."

"I have visited an abattoir, mom," I remind her. "You took me to one on my fifth birthday, remember?" She frowns, trying to recall, but I save her the trouble and change the subject. "How have you been?"

"I'm heartbroken."

"Again?"

"Yes. Dinah left me. It's why I've been battling to sleep."

"Which one is Dinah again?"

"The redhead. Freckles. Legs that go up to here." She lifts a hand to well above her waistline and waits for me to register.

"Ah, yes, Dinah," I say knowingly. "Wasn't she married?"

"Not happily. Her husband doesn't understand her."

"That's what they all say, mom."

"Not all of them. Besides, in Dinah's case, it's true. The husband's a complete dickhead."

"You can't know that for sure," I say, smiling up at the waitress who's arrived back at the table with our coffees. "You've only heard her side of the story."

"Nuh-uh," she says, adding two heaped teaspoons of sugar to her coffee. "I've heard his too. They attended one of Barbara's cooking classes. The bastard spent the entire evening trying to stick his hand up my skirt."

I choke on my coffee. "He what?"

"Well, to be fair, I dated him first."

"Mom!"

"What? Honey, there are a lot of unhappy people out there. And this was before I knew Dinah, obviously." She shakes her head, and I feel as though I've been reprimanded. I should be used to it by now – my mother's warped sense of reasoning.

"Jesus mom, it's no wonder I'm so screwed up."

She gives me a look of utter bewilderment. "Screwed up? What on earth are you going on about, Cat? You're the most well-adjusted person I know." Given the company my mother typically keeps, I can't say I find that very reassuring.

I go almost an entire month without seeing Aaron. My routine is my undoing. I'm at the coffee shop, hard at work, when a warm body slides into the booth beside me.

Aaron's lips pull upward. "Hello, stranger."

"What the hell are you doing here?" I hiss, casting a furtive look around.

"We need to talk." For once, he makes no attempt to touch me, folding his hands instead on the table before him, lean fingers steepled. His eyes are bruised, as if he hasn't been getting enough sleep, and he looks younger, somehow – more vulnerable, without the smug smile he normally wears.

"About what?" I ask.

"About us." A plain and simple answer, no snide remark or cocky comeback.

"There is no us, Aaron."

"That's not true, and you know it."

With a sigh, I snap my MacBook shut. "We're separated. It's time we started acting like it."

"I miss you." He says it with a straight face and doesn't back down even when I arch my brows at him, calling his bluff.

"I can't keep doing this, Aaron. I can't be your bit on the side. It's not fair to Blake. Or Staci," I add as an afterthought.

"Do you remember that trip we took to Lake Como?"

It's an abrupt change of subject, but I go along with it. "How could I forget?"

We'd spent ten days in Italy, one Christmas. We'd randomly chosen Lake Como off an ultimate holidays website, and we'd booked tickets that same night. Aaron's parents had been less than thrilled. They preferred us to spend Christmas with them, but given that the invitation was never extended to my mother, I didn't feel half as guilty as I should have about flying off to Italy instead.

"I still can't pass a boat shop without remembering that boat ride."

I arch my brow at him again. The boat ride had hardly been romantic. Out in the middle of the lake, we'd tried to make whoopie, and ended up falling in.

"Oh, come on," he teases, catching sight of my expression. "It was funny."

"It was cold."

"We had good times, Cat."

"We had bad times too. Or, maybe you would still call those good times, given that you were the one having all the fun."

"You know I never meant to hurt you."

"You could've fooled me." I tap my fingers on the table. "Look, I have work to do. And I don't have time for a trip up memory lane. Why are you here, Aaron?"

"I love you."

It comes so completely out of the blue that I can't help the incredulous expression which plasters itself on my face.

"What?"

"I love you."

I shake my head, disarmed by his open gaze. "No you don't. If you loved me, we wouldn't be in this situation."

He exhales a long breath. "Cat, we're different. We don't work the usual way, and I'm not going to bother trying to pretend that we do. But I *do* love you, and I want you in my life."

"You want a booty call," I correct.

His face darkens. "And you don't?"

"What is that supposed to mean?"

"Oh come on, Cat. We're both adults here. Love doesn't always conquer the demon. And we're both just a little bit fucked up. Blame our parents, daddy issues, whatever you want, but don't try to deny that you need me as much as I need you."

I don't even bother to argue. I'm not a hypocrite, and the fact is that I've answered every time he's summoned. I want to call him out on the daddy issues comment, given that his father is a successful businessman named Stan, who just celebrated his thirty-fifth wedding anniversary, but what would be the point? I already know I'm screwed up, and it's likely my mom and absentee father have a lot to do with it.

"Need isn't the same thing as love," I say instead, but I can feel that old magic working. My treacherous heart, responding to his words.

"For us, it is."

I knead my temples as the waitress returns to check if Aaron wants anything. Amy isn't here today, thank the stars.

"I'm okay, thank you. Cat...?" I shake my head, and he waves her away. His hand brushes my shoulder, softly, briefly, and then it's gone. "I know this is messed up," he admits. "I know you've moved on." He swallows as if just speaking the words pains him. "I have too, but I just can't stay away from you. I've tried, but I can't."

I lift my eyes to his. I feel hollow. "Did you ever think maybe there's a reason for that? That maybe we're meant to be together – that we should try to work things out?"

He holds my gaze, doesn't flinch away from the question. The corners of his mouth twitch. He raises his hand to toy with a strand of my hair, and I close my eyes, lost in the moment, forgetting where I am and who might be watching.

"Can you honestly tell me you think that'll work?" he whispers.

"I can honestly tell you that I don't want to hurt anyone else."

He smiles then, finally, but it's still not the cruel smile he usually wears. "Cat, I didn't ever want to hurt you in the first place."

I pull away from him, needing to put some distance between us. I'd been ready to end things, I was tired and angry at being used, but I'm utterly unprepared for this emotional onslaught. To my amazement, he doesn't push it. Instead, he gets to his feet and gazes down at me.

"Come home with me." His voice is barely more than a whisper. "Let me show you how much you mean to me."

Reality snaps back into place, leaving me reeling. "It's Friday," I sneer, giving a bitter laugh. "I should have known."

"That's not what this is about," Aaron snaps. "I want to remind you why we're so good together."

"Go to hell."

He holds my gaze for a few seconds and then lowers his eyes. "This isn't over."

"I want it to be over."

For a second, the smug look flits across his face. "No, you don't."

WHEN HE'S GONE I twitch in agitation, the sense that things have been left unfinished keeping me from concentrating. Hating myself, I pack up my things and hail a cab.

Aaron opens the door almost immediately. His face splits into a smile that is nothing short of dazzling. I open my mouth to speak, but a sob bursts from my chest instead. His strong arms come around me, leading me inside and onto the couch. He holds me until my body stops heaving, and my tears have run dry. Then he lowers his head and kisses me, softly, sweetly, as if I might break apart at any minute.

His lips brush the tears from my eyes, his hands stroke my hair, my shoulders, the small of my back. I've never known him to be so tender, and when his hands reach for my buttons, I don't stop him. When I'm naked from the waist up, he stops, leaning back to admire the view. He cups my chin, lifting it so I have to meet his eyes.

"Are you sure?" he asks. I wish he hadn't. It's easier to play the victim. I nod, my chin rubbing gently against his palm. I know what this means. He's made himself very clear. There will be no reconciliation, not now, at least. But I still feel the thrill of the hold I have over him, the rush of the physical connection between us. And he's right – I *do* need it.

Slowly, leisurely, Aaron torments me with his intimate teasing, caressing me until I'm feverish with desire. When I can't take another second of it, knowing full well I'm going to hate myself later but not giving a damn, I seize hold of his arms and dig my nails in deep. His lips part against mine in a wicked, knowing smile, and his breath quickens. For the first time, he doesn't object when I rake his skin, leaving red marks in my wake. Free to do whatever I want, I meet his passion with abandon.

Two hours later, I stagger from Aaron's apartment, my body tender but absolutely sated. Aaron texts me the next day to say he loves me. And the day after that. And the day after that. I text it back, but I don't break things off with Blake. I'm weak. Weak and gullible. But I'm not stupid.

7

It's a typical Californian spring day – mild and warm and uneventful – when Blake finds my stash of paintings in the loft. Blake had the day off, and I'd had to go see a client who wanted to completely revamp his online store.

"You really should just leave that here," I'd told him that morning, catching sight of the overflowing suitcase at the foot of my bed. "Why don't you clear out some space in my closet and keep some of your stuff here? That way you won't have to live out of a suitcase."

His smile had been worth it. Since I'd reignited my affair with Aaron, I'd been more distant and Blake, intuitive as he is, had noticed. There was a disconnect between us that hadn't been there before. It was ironic because the more time I spent with him, the more my feelings for him grew, but so did my guilt at what I was doing. I'd left him with a lingering kiss and free rein to re-organize my closet. The meeting had gone on longer than I expected, and by the time I got back home, I'd forgotten all about it.

I drop my purse on the kitchen counter to find Blake looking puzzled, and a little perturbed. He's holding the nude I bought last month.

"Please tell me this isn't Janine," he says. I can only imagine how awkward it must be for him to see one of the duty nurses he works with, in all her pink-fleshed glory, but I'm too angry to care. All the insecurities I had when I was with Aaron rear their ugly heads. And it doesn't matter that Blake isn't Aaron, because my embarrassment can't differentiate between the two.

"Where did you find that?"

"In the loft. I figured I'd move your winter stuff up there – I boxed it, but when I went up I found this. And a bunch of others, all with the price tags still attached," he adds meaningfully. "They're your moms, right?" he frowns at the flamboyant signature in the bottom corner to confirm it. "Babe, why are you buying your mother's paintings?"

"That's none of your business."

He flinches at the harsh tone of my voice. "Hey, I wasn't prying. I'm sorry, I just..." His eyes flicker between me and the painting. "I didn't mean to upset you," he finishes softly.

I snatch the painting back and try to rewrap it, but I only end up tearing the brown wrapping paper in half.

Blake halts me with a firm hand on mine. Our gazes lock.

"Stop it," he says.

"I try to wrench my hand away, but he closes his fingers over mine in a vice grip.

"Let me go."

"No."

"I said, let me go!" I yank my hand away so violently he staggers. "You have no right to be snooping through my stuff!" I'm yelling, but I've grown so used to having to defend my mother that *defensive* has become my default setting where she's concerned.

Blake doesn't respond. Calmly, he retrieves the painting with his free hand and sets it on the couch, facing away from us. When he turns back to me, his amber eyes have lost their usual warmth. "I can't do this anymore."

"You can't do what?" I lower my voice as an inkling of dread spiders down my spine.

"Keep chipping away at your walls. What is this, Cat?" He waves his hand between the two of us. "Because I can tell you right now, it's not a relationship."

"People fight, Blake. It's not abnormal."

"We don't fight. You don't care enough to fight. You just shut down and shut me out." In all the time we've spent together, I've never seen this side of him – the unyielding strength, the unwavering confidence.

"Shut you out? You're practically living here, how is that shutting you out?"

He regards me levelly and his question, when it comes, throws me into turmoil.

"When are you going to file for a divorce?" I trip over my next words, and Blake holds up his hand for me to stop talking. "I think that's answer enough. We've been dating almost six months, and yet, you're still married. Don't you think that's just a bit fucked up?"

If only you knew, I find myself thinking hysterically. Still, my heart is thundering in my chest. I don't know what's happening, but I have a sinking sensation that Blake might be about to break up with me. More surprisingly, the thought crucifies me.

"I don't know what you want me to say," I mumble.

"Well then, let me help you." He raises his hands and cups my face. "I love you, Cat. I'm sorry I didn't say it sooner, but I didn't know if you were ready. Now I don't know if you ever will be. This isn't some random fling, not to me. You're the most infuriating woman I've ever met, but I can't help myself." He squeezes his eyes shut for just a moment, and when he opens them, I want to weep with relief that a bit of warmth has seeped back. "I love you," he echoes, "and call me selfish, but I want all of you. I want to help you, to heal you, and to bring you back from the hell that bastard put you through, but I can't do that if you won't let me in. And I can't stay here anymore and watch you self-destruct, because it'll destroy me, too."

I blink up at him, trying to process what this means, to process the bomb he's just dropped on me and the best way to respond. I don't know if I love Blake. I know I don't want to lose him, but does that equate to love?

My hesitation is too much. His face is scrunched in pain and embarrassment as he moves away from me, toward the door. He doesn't even bother to collect his things.

"Blake!"

"No, Cat." He wards me off. "No more. I can't do this. I'm done."

I stare at the door for a full minute after it closes behind him. *What the hell have I done?* I don't even know I've spoken the words aloud, until they ring hollow in my ears. As if in a trance, I slump onto the couch, my thoughts hurtling around my head a mile a minute as I try to imagine my life without Blake in it. It's unimaginably painful. I've been so caught up in my affair with Aaron, I've underestimated how important Blake has become to me, how steadfast and dependable. And let's face it, dependable isn't sexy, but now that he's gone, I'm wracked with regret. I'm also angry – furious that he didn't give me time to explain before he stormed out. *Not that you deserve it*, a snide voice in my head sneers.

I think I'm going to throw up.

No, you're not.

I don't know what to do.

Yes, you do.

"No." I speak the word aloud, determined to ignore the driving need to chase after Blake and beg him to come back. It's better this way. I've treated him appallingly, and it's obvious I don't have the strength to break things off with Aaron, so why should Blake suffer any more than he has. Decision made, I walk slowly to my room to pack up his things.

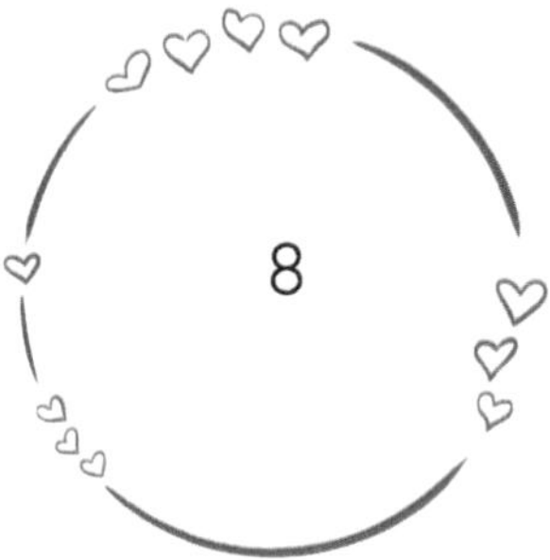

8

"Why aren't you eating?" My mother demands three days later when I meet her for breakfast. I've barely eaten a thing since Blake walked out, but I don't tell her that. I still can't believe that the same day Blake finally told me he loved me, our relationship ended. It doesn't seem fair, but considering that I only realized just how strongly I felt for him around the same time, I've accepted that my timing is disastrous.

"I had a big breakfast," I lie, curling my hands around my mug for warmth. Living almost exclusively on caffeine is ill-advised, judging by the way my hands are shaking, and I slosh a liberal amount of coffee over the table.

"Cat!" my mother scolds, pulling a grubby looking tissue from her bag to mop it up. A small handful of greenish-brown flutters onto the table. "Oh, shit, I forgot that was in there. It's medicinal," she tells the waiter, as he darts forward to clean up the mess. He gives me a secret wink, but I'm too drained to react. I'm tired of my mother's outlandish behavior – of the shitty example she sets, and the secrets she keeps from me. I don't like the person I've become. Not one bit. And if I'm going to be better, I need answers. It's time for me and

Viola to have a serious conversation. I steel myself and prepare to ask the question that is the entire reason I invited her here in the first place.

"Mom." I make sure I have her undivided attention before I continue. "I want to know who my father is."

Her expression is almost comical. A mixture of shock and bewilderment, with a healthy dose of outrage. Being Viola, however, it doesn't take long for her to recover.

"Why on earth would you care?" she snaps. "He abandoned me the second he heard I was pregnant."

"He abandoned *you*," I point out. "And I get that in doing so he abandoned me too, but I should be allowed to make my own judgment. I can't do that without even knowing who he is." I've thought about this for days. I never wanted to meet my father, or at least, I thought I didn't, but now a part of me suspects my decision may have been my mother's all along. Her influence over me, her insistence that my father is the devil who doesn't deserve us. I never even thought to question it, not until now.

"You don't want to meet him, Cat. He's no good for you."

"Again, that's my decision to make."

"He's dead."

I arch my brow and call her bluff. "Mom."

"Fine, he's not dead, but he may as well be, for all the good he's done you."

I stare her down, and she starts to squirm.

"Please, baby, don't do this. Am I not enough? Because I've dedicated my whole life to you." I want to laugh at the absurdity of that statement, but I don't, because I know that she needs to believe the lie.

"Mom, I love you. This has nothing to do with you and me, but I need to know who he is. I need to know where I came from. I'm not going to be able to truly find myself until I do."

"Find yourself? You're not lost, Cat. You've got a great job, a beautiful home, and you're dating a surgeon. I'd say you're leaps and bounds ahead of most girls your age. Hell, I knew both my parents and I'm far more screwed up than you are."

"Jesus, mom!" I get to my feet, a wave of anger and helplessness surging through me. "This isn't about *you,* okay? Not everything is about you!"

Now she's playing it right up, her eyes wide and wounded, one hand over her heart, the other surreptitiously reaching for the rolled joint peeking out of her purse like a security blanket. For a second I wonder if she might actually bring it out and light up right here at the table.

"Have I done something wrong, Cat?" she asks in a tiny, breathless voice. It's an act – always the act. "Are you trying to hurt me?"

And just like that, I know that she is never going to tell me. She's never going to take responsibility, never understand how badly I need to know the truth. It will never, ever be about me. Disgusted, I toss enough money on the table to cover our bill, including a generous tip, while my mother sits in stunned silence. "I can't do this right now," I say in a voice like acid.

I make it halfway to the door before I turn back. "Oh, and about that surgeon you love so much? He *left* me. He left me because as much as you hate to admit it, I *am* screwed up." I wait until she raises her eyes to mine. "I guess I really am my mother's daughter."

"Oh, honey"

"No." I cut her off before her sympathy pushes me over the edge. "You don't get to talk to me about it. You don't get to say you're sorry for me, and try to make me feel better, because it's your fault as well as mine." Yes, I screwed up. Yes, Blake was right to leave me. But she's a part of the reason I'm such a mess, and I'll be damned if I let her get away with it any longer. "Don't contact me," I say coldly. "I don't want to hear from you until you're ready to tell me the truth."

I hear her call my name as I walk away but I don't look back. If I'm going to pick up the pieces of my broken life, I'm starting right now.

. . .

OUT ON THE STREET, I suck in a huge breath of air, trying to rid myself of the smell of ketchup and cooking oil. My legs are trembling so badly it takes me a few seconds before I risk stepping up to the curb. Casting quick glances over my shoulder, terrified that my mother might still come after me, I flag down the first taxi I see and launch myself into the back seat. I'm giving the driver directions before I've even closed the door.

Breaking the cardinal rule of mine and Aaron's relationship, I go straight to his apartment. I don't phone first. If Staci is home, I'll just pretend there's been a death in the family. That's a good enough reason for me to contact him. I slump in the backseat of the cab and replay the conversation with my mother. The cab driver gives me a concerned look as I hand over the cash, but says nothing. I stumble into Aaron's building, bolting the two flights of stairs to his floor. He greets me at the door wearing only a pair of faded jeans and a shirt which is unbuttoned, baring his bronzed chest. He probably only pulled it on to answer the door.

"Sweetheart," he croons, the second he lays eyes on me quivering in the hall, "I wasn't expecting you."

"Is she here?"

"No."

I shove past him, into the apartment. The TV is on low, and Aaron's hair is still damp from a recent shower. "Did you just get up?"

He shrugs, then reaches for me. "You know I'm not a morning person. Although, now that you're here, I could definitely become one. To what do I owe the honor?"

I lean into him, letting his hands knead all the tension out of me. When we kiss, he tastes of coffee. Behind him, I see two naked women on the screen, and the scent of incense lingers in the air. I shut my eyes and block it all out, reaching for his straining zipper. I know of one way to numb the pain, and I'm not leaving here until I get it. Quick as a flash, Aaron steps out of my reach.

"What's the hurry, Kitty Cat?" He's teasing now, another game to be played. There's no mistaking the wicked glint in his eyes. I look up at him and burst into tears.

Aaron is at my side in an instant, drawing me to the couch. "What is it?" he asks, confusion etched on his brow. "What's wrong?"

It all comes out; the altercation with my mother, the unanswered questions about my father, Blake leaving me. I tell him how I feel like I'm stuck in an endless spin cycle, getting nowhere. I'm so absorbed in my own grief that I barely notice when his weight shifts, until the arm that was around my shoulders slowly withdraws.

"Baby, you're being too hard on yourself."

I gaze up at him, studying his face. He looks uncomfortable. He looks as though he doesn't want to be here.

"What are you doing?" I ask, as the tears dry on my cheeks.

"What do you mean?"

"I came here because I thought you would understand. Because you're the one person in the world who really knows me. Why are you backpedaling?"

"I'm not backpedaling! I'm right here."

I narrow my eyes at him, trying to pinpoint the source of my unease.

"Oh my God!" I clap a hand to my mouth as it hits me like a ton of bricks. "You son of a bitch!" He gets to his feet the same time I do. "You're actually *upset* that he dumped me, aren't you?"

"What? Of course not!" His eyes tell a different story.

"You really don't give a shit about me, do you? It's all just a sick game to you! You got your rocks off precisely because Blake was in the picture, not because you had feelings for me. This was all a game of fucking one-upmanship."

"That's ridiculous. Are you even listening to yourself?"

I swipe furiously at the tears still drying on my cheeks. "God, I've been such a fool. You don't want me, Aaron, you just don't want anyone else to have me."

"Cat, you need to calm down. I didn't make you any promises, remember? And in case you've forgotten, I didn't seduce you into coming here. You came to me."

This time, the tears that spring to my eyes are tears of shame. "You're right, I did. Because you're an escape, Aaron. A beautiful, twisted escape. But I never escape, do I? I just end up back in the same shitty hole."

When I arrive at the hospital, Blake is in surgery. To my mortification, Janine is the head nurse on duty, but she at least knows who I am, and she offers to let me wait in one of the on-call rooms, which I'm sure isn't really allowed. I wait for over an hour before Blake appears, wearing the tired but triumphant expression I've come to recognize as a sign of a successful surgery. It breaks my heart that his euphoria diminishes when he catches sight of me. He removes his scrub cap and leans back against the door in resignation.

"Janine told me you were here." He says it as though he had tried to convince himself she was lying, and is bitterly disappointed to find that it's true.

"I'm sorry to come while you're working," I begin hesitantly, "but this couldn't wait." His only response is a wave of his hand, letting me know to continue. "Look, I know I messed up. There are *so* many ways I messed up, and so many things I wish I had done differently, but I can't change any of that." I take a breath and two small steps toward him. "I came here to tell you that I love you. Wait, let me finish," I add quickly when he opens his mouth to speak. "I don't want us to get back together. Not yet, anyway. You don't deserve this. I don't deserve you, not the way I am now. You were right about everything – I do shut you out. But I want to be better, I'm *going* to be better. And hopefully, when that time comes, maybe you might consider trying again. If you haven't been swept off your feet by some gorgeous patient who realizes how amazing you are," I add, trying to lighten the mood.

Blake doesn't smile. He regards me thoughtfully. "I'm sorry, Cat, but as much as I appreciate the honesty, I still don't understand why you're here."

"I buy my mother's paintings because when she's working she's sober," I blurt out. "Not for long, but long enough that I get to spend a few hours with her. With the real her – not the junkie who barely notices I'm around."

"Okay, but"

"I'm not done," I say quickly, terrified I'll lose my nerve if I don't get it all out. "I haven't divorced Aaron because deep down I'm afraid no one else would want me."

He doesn't let that one slide. "*I* wanted you. You know I did." The past tense hurts, but I keep going.

"How can you want someone if you don't really know who they are?" I counter.

He lets loose an exasperated sigh. "What exactly is it that you want from me? What more do I need to do to prove myself to you?"

I smile, even as a tear slips over my lashes and down my cheek. "It's not you who needs to prove yourself."

Blake has never seen me cry. More importantly, it's in his nature to care for people in pain. At the sight of my tears, he moves, crossing the distance between us in a single stride, and pulls me against his chest.

"Please don't cry," he murmurs into my hair. "Please. Just tell me what to do, Cat, and I'll do it."

I raise my head. "Please don't leave me. Don't give up on me. Not yet."

His shoulders go rigid. "Cat"

"I mean it. I'm a mess, but I love you, and I'm going to prove it."

"How?"

I give him a watery-eyed smile. "Well, for starters, I'd like you to come with me to see a divorce attorney."

BLAKE COMES over to my apartment straight from work and helps me search for a list of divorce attorneys within a ten-mile radius. I pick one at random and save the number to my phone.

"You're sure about this?" he asks. He's keeping his distance. I'd meant what I said – I won't mess up again. When and if Blake and I get back together, I want it to be for good, and until Aaron is out of my life, I know I can't be one hundred percent honest with him.

"I'm sure. I'll call first thing in the morning. I just want my life back."

"I'm proud of you," he says. He's also promised to help me try to track down my father. We spend the rest of the evening scrolling through the website of the college my mom attended, paying particular attention to the professors who worked there the year before I was born. I examine each and every face, but I can find no trace of myself in any of them.

"It's impossible to tell," Blake sighs, leaning back and rolling his shoulders. "People claim their kids look like them, but honestly, half the time it's bullshit. I can't tell you how many times I've complimented a mother on her kid and how they look just like her, only to discover she's the step-parent." He squints back at the screen, but I shake my head.

"You're right. This isn't going to work."

"Maybe your mom will come clean?" he says hopefully.

"I doubt it. She's had twenty-four years to do that."

"Okay, what about your grandparents? Surely they'd know something."

"Even if they did, I don't know if they'd tell me. They're super-conservative, and terrified of my mother."

"You can only try."

"True." I check my watch. "It's too late to call. I'll do it in the morning."

"You should probably go and see them," he warns. "Something this sensitive... well, you might have better luck in person."

I give him a teasing smile. "How did you get so smart?"

"It's a gift." He grins.

I can tell that Blake is as loath as I am to let the evening end, but I force myself to get to my feet and walk him to the door. He takes one step into the hall and then turns back to face me.

"I don't have to go," he says, the words coming out in a rush. "I have clothes here. I could sleep in the spare room and... or not," he adds, catching sight of the look on my face.

"I wish you could," I moan, and he knows that I mean it. "But if you stay, there's no way I'd be able to leave you alone in the spare room."

A ridiculously smug smile creases his face, and I laugh out loud.

"I miss you," he murmurs when I've recovered.

On a whim, I step forward and kiss his cheek, breathing in the familiar smell of his aftershave. "I miss you too." It would be so easy to reach for him, to bring him back inside and pick up where we left off, but I summon every ounce of my willpower and let him go. Blake is worth waiting for. I won't screw this up again.

FIRST THING THE FOLLOWING MORNING, I call the attorney's office to schedule a meeting. As luck would have it, they have a cancellation in the afternoon, and I take it without hesitation. I text Blake to let him know, but he has a surgery lined up later. I can tell by the tone of his text that he feels bad about it.

You have lives to save, I send back, *I've got this*. Then, without calling first to let them know I'm coming, I drive out to the suburbs to ambush my grandparents.

My mother's parents live in a gorgeous Tudor home with a white picket fence entirely smothered in climbing roses. It's a picture-book house, singularly inappropriate for the woman who grew up here. I arrive to find my grandmother, Francine, alone in the house, my grandfather having already left for his weekly round of golf.

"Catrina, sweetheart, what a lovely surprise!" My grandmother says when she answers the bell to find me standing at the door. "Why didn't you tell me you were coming down? I would've made some scones." My grandmother is the type of woman who would die before presenting a guest with store-bought confectionaries.

"Sorry, Grams." I wipe my boots on the doormat, freeing them of any invisible dirt she might discover. "It was a last minute thing."

"Well, we'll have to make do with some shortbread. I made some yesterday, you know how your grandpa loves it."

Ensconced in the enormous kitchen, armed with a cup of hot, sweet tea and a plate piled high with shortbread, I launch my attack.

"Grams, I need to know who my father is."

Her lips disappear into a disapproving line, and it's a while before she speaks. "May I ask why?"

"I wouldn't think you'd need to," I reply. Grams possesses the reasonable logic my mother lacks. Any child would want to know – it's a measure of how deep my mother's manipulation runs that I haven't until now. Grams locks her fingers around the tear-shaped ruby at her throat, and twists it. "I know it's not an easy subject," I say gently, "but I really need to know. If you won't tell me I'll go to her campus and start asking around, which would be a thousand times worse, but if that's what it takes, then that's what I'll do. Please, Grams, just tell me. I have a right to know."

"Your mother"

"My mother doesn't get to choose for me! I'm a grown woman, I've earned the right to decide for myself. Mom made a mistake not telling me and deep down, I think you know that."

"I know," she sighs, releasing the ruby. "I've told your Pop for years that it was only a matter of time before you came looking for answers, but your mom made us promise to never discuss it with you."

"Why?"

Her eyes are downcast. "Because she's ashamed."

"That she was seduced by a professor? He's the one who should be ashamed. He's the one who took advantage of a vulnerable young girl."

The second I say it, I know it's a lie. Grams' eyes tell me so before her lips even move.

"Sweetheart, your father wasn't a college professor." I hold my breath, not daring to speak in case she changes her mind. Grams gets up and puts the kettle back on even though we've barely touched our tea. "When your mother went off to college, she met another student – a lovely girl from a very respectable family. I was thrilled, obviously. Your mom had already been in some trouble at school and I thought Sophie would be a good influence on her." By her tone, I gather that wasn't the case. No doubt the opposite happened, and poor Sophie was led astray by my feckless mother. "In their second year, the girls had a falling out. I wasn't sure at the time what had happened, and your mother refused to talk about it."

"How very unlike her," I say, barely concealing the sarcasm in my voice. Grams gives a small, dissatisfied sigh, and sets a fresh cup of tea next to my rapidly cooling first cup. "Then we discovered your mother was pregnant."

"Was he Sophie's boyfriend?" I ask, trying to connect the dots. It's nothing less than I'd expect of my mother at this point, to try to hurt her previous friend in the worst way imaginable.

"No," Grams shakes her greying head. "Her younger brother, Stephen."

"Okay," I say, not understanding what all the fuss was about. Grams has already said that Sophie came from a respectable family. "So why wouldn't anyone tell me this?"

It takes her a moment to drum up the courage to speak. "He was only sixteen at the time." All the air seems to drain from my chest, but Grams is on a roll now, a runaway train with no brakes. "I contacted Sophie's parents when I learned the truth, but they wanted nothing to do with it. They even threatened to charge your mother with statutory assault, but that was just a knee-jerk reaction. The Bennetts didn't want the scandal any more than we did, and it was obvious that Stephen had been a willing participant. He admitted later that your mother wasn't his first." She shifts on her chair, uncomfortable at the mention of all this implied sex, but I pay no heed. I'm too busy doing the math in my head. If Stephen was sixteen when I was conceived, that would make him around forty now, forty-one at most.

"I get why this is such a sensitive subject," I say slowly, trying to invoke more understanding than I really feel, "but that doesn't explain why he wanted nothing to do with me."

"Oh Cat," Grams' eyes are starting to water. Her hands are back at her throat, twisting the ruby so tightly I fear the chain might snap. "He never knew you existed. His parents refused to tell him. They paid your mother quite a large sum of money to... well, to take care of things, not that it was necessary, and she dropped out right after."

"They wanted her to terminate the pregnancy? Without even telling him about it?"

"Yes. But your mother never once considered it," she adds quickly, as if that decision alone redeems my mother from a lifetime of shitty parenting.

"And she never thought to let him know? To tell them to hell with their money and tell him anyway?" I find it hard to believe that my mother would follow anyone's instructions, let alone the wealthy parents of a man she'd been involved with. Then again, there was cash involved. I drop my head into my hands, trying to make sense of it.

"Viola wouldn't have told Stephen anyway," she says, and I raise my head. "He'd met someone else, you see, and your mother's never taken rejection kindly. I don't think even Sophie knew the truth. After that," Gram continues, "your mother went from bad to worse. She was sober throughout her pregnancy," she adds, putting a reassuring hand on my arm, "your Pop and I made sure of that. But once you were born she... well, you know how she is."

"I do," I whisper. On autopilot, I get up and set both cups in the sink, watching as the tannin-colored liquid pools around the drain. "I have to go, Grams."

"Don't leave, Catrina. This must be such a shock. You should stay, I'm happy to answer any questions you might have." There's a new determination in her voice. I want to smile at the tiny act of rebellion against my mother, but my cheeks are frozen.

"I'm fine, Grams. Thank you for telling me, but I really have to go."

"What are you going to do?"

"I don't know," I lie. "I need time to process it all."

"Well, whatever you decide, sweetheart, I'm here for you. And I'm sorry that I didn't tell you before. You're right, you deserve the truth."

I walk out to my car in a daze. I finally have a name. Stephen Bennett.

10

I barely register what the attorney is saying as I sit through the hour-long meeting. I answer his questions on autopilot. My finances, Aaron's finances, the marital property, how and why the marriage ended – nothing is sacrosanct. When the questions finally cease, he gets me to sign the paperwork which will initiate divorce proceedings and promises that Aaron will be served within five business days. I feel like a weight has been lifted off my shoulders, but I'm too numb to appreciate it.

For the rest of the week, I spend my evenings eating junk food, binge-watching Netflix, and stalking Sophie and Stephen Bennett online. I text Blake every time I discover something new, and he replies with enthusiasm. Stephen doesn't have a Facebook page, but Sophie does. She's Sophie Walker now, but her maiden name is still shown on her profile, and I assume it's her because we have a mutual friend in my mother's friend Barbara, who attended the same art school. I scan through the few photographs that are public, but find only a man with an impressive beard and smiling eyes. He's kissing her cheek in one of the pictures, so I figure he's her husband, not her brother. Sophie works at a company called Bennett Communications. A quick Google search tells me it's been in operation for almost four decades. If it's a family firm, and given the name, I can only assume it is, it's highly possible that my father works there too. I consider contacting Sophie through her Facebook profile, but decide against it. This isn't something I can do on Messenger. The address listed for Bennett Communications is in Long Beach. It's a six-hour drive at least, so I decide to drive up over the weekend, spend some time on my own, and confront Stephen Bennett at his office on Monday morning. When I text Blake to inform him of my plans, he insists on taking the weekend off to come with me.

Do you think that's a good idea? I ask, my heart in my throat at the thought of spending an entire weekend alone with him. His answering text is short and decisive: *You're not doing this on your own.*

ON FRIDAY MORNING, I pack our bags. Now that I've had a few days to get used to the idea, I'm excited about spending a whole weekend alone with Blake, away from everything and everyone, especially Aaron. As if my thoughts had summoned him, I find a text from Aaron on my phone, asking if we can meet. Staci has seriously got to stop working on Fridays. I'm assuming he hasn't received the papers, and I don't reply. It's becoming surprisingly easy to ignore him.

Blake drives a dark blue pick-up. It's very comfortable, far more so than my little run around Volkswagen. We have a six-hour journey ahead, broken only by a brief stop for lunch, and I'm subjected to the sight of Blake's long, lean legs stretched out beside me for far longer than I can bear. My hand itches to touch his denim-clad thigh, so I clench my fists and focus on the road. Blake, meanwhile, makes easy conversation, seemingly unaffected by the close proximity. It doesn't do much for my ego.

We arrive at the Air B&B, aptly named *Step Right Inn*, an hour before check-in. The owner is a sweet, middle-aged woman named Alice, who has the curliest hair I've ever seen. It's frizzed as though she stuck her finger in an electrical outlet, but her smile is warm, and her blue eyes twinkle as she ushers us into the bar for a drink while we wait.

"Your room is almost ready," she promises, offering us a complimentary glass of cheap sherry beside a crackling fire, despite the stifling heat of the day. Being polite, Blake takes one sip while she watches, hides his grimace, and smiles instead. The second she's out of the room, he sets the glass on the counter.

"Jesus, I think I just seared my stomach lining."

I giggle and set my own glass down without taking a single sip. "That bad?"

"Worse." He takes a seat on the couch and whips off his jumper. The temperature in the room seems to go up a few degrees, and it has nothing to do with the fire. Awkwardly, I perch on the opposite edge. As the sound of a Hoover starts up somewhere above us, Blake gives me a lazy smile.

"Are you going to spend the next seventy-two hours curled up like a frightened kitten?" he asks.

"Maybe," I admit. "I'm starting to think this might not have been the best idea."

"Why?" he teases, "because you're worried you won't be able to keep your hands off me?"

"Yes."

It's not the answer he expected. Slowly, he stretches out his arm, inch by inch, until it lies along the top of the couch. Then he curls his finger and beckons me closer. "Come here." I shake my head, but he only smiles and shifts up until he's right beside me. My heart flip-flops in my chest.

"What are we doing, Cat?"

"We're on a mission," I remind him, deliberately ignoring his meaning. "To find my father and get answers." His scent is assaulting my senses. I try to get up, but he grabs my hand, pulling me back.

"Don't," I warn.

"Why?"

"Because," I begin, but then I catch sight of the way that he's looking at me and every argument I could possibly come up with dies on my lips.

"What are we doing?" he repeats.

"I don't know."

"This is ridiculous. You told me you love me."

"I do."

"And you know I'm in love with you?"

I bob my head.

"Then why in God's name are we torturing ourselves?"

My lack of response is all the invitation he needs. When he pulls me onto his lap, I can't help myself. I gasp. Blake's eyes widen, and then narrow almost instantly. I duck my head, not wanting him to see the blush creeping up my neck and across my cheeks.

"There's something I haven't told you yet," I mumble.

"I'm listening."

My voice is small and breathless. "Sometimes I like things a little bit wilder than most women."

His fingers find my chin, tilt my head back. His eyes are hooded, but I feel like he can see into the depths of my soul.

"Wilder?" he asks, still not understanding.

"Sex," I whisper, mortified that I have to explain. "I'm not depraved. Or perverted," I add quickly. "I'm not into threesomes, or porn, or..." I trail off, too embarrassed to vocalize some of the things he might be thinking. "I just like sex. A lot. And sometimes I like to take a few risks..." I can't go on. A hard, dry lump has formed in my throat and I can't get anything else out.

He drops my chin, and I cringe, waiting for the hammer to fall. I knew this would change how he saw me, but there's no going back. I promised myself I would be one hundred percent honest from now on. The reason I'm so drawn to Aaron is that he understands this side of me. I'll never get as close to any other man so long as I keep them in the dark.

Blake is silent for the longest time.

"What kind of risks?" he asks eventually.

"Just risks," I croak. His hand moves to the waistband of my tights, and I hold my breath. He skims the thin fabric, but doesn't stop, moving lower until his hand cups my ass cheek. His grip tightens.

"What risks?" he repeats, his voice low and husky. He breathes the words into my ear, and I shiver, involuntarily.

Blake's eyes rise to the ceiling, where the sound of the Hoover is a distant hum, and I close my own as comprehension dawns on him. When I open them, his lips are curved upward. It's a wicked smile. Still holding me in his lap, he rises from the couch and crosses to the bar. His face is impossible to read as he deposits me onto one of the bar stools and pours himself a scotch. He takes only a small sip. When he offers me the glass, I down it, the amber liquid scorching a trail down my throat.

Blake's fingers slide down my arms and over my thighs, until he reaches my knees. He forces them apart, quickly, deliberately, and steps into the space between them. I'm too terrified to move. I don't know what he's doing, but my pulse quickens. My hands ache to touch him, but when I reach for him, he swats them away.

"What are you doing?" I whisper.

He cocks his head to one side and regards me levelly. "I'm offended, Cat," he says, his eyes homing in on my mouth. He leans forward and runs his tongue across my lower lip before catching it briefly between his teeth. "I studied the human anatomy," he murmurs, his breath filling my mouth. "You should have had a little more faith in me."

With every word, his fingers are circling my thighs, inching upward, and my body unravels just that little bit more. Somewhere in my addled brain, I'm aware that the Hoover is still going, but there's nothing to say that someone won't walk right through the door at any second. Still, I arch my back, exposing my throat and pressing my hips toward his probing fingers.

Blake doesn't hesitate. Lifting me off the chair, setting me down on trembling legs, he whips down my tights and my underwear in one swift movement. He takes a second to release his zipper, then seizes my hips and lifts me clear off the ground. I give a cry of ecstasy as he rams himself into me, my head dropping back, exposing my neck to his mouth. Upstairs, the Hoover falls silent, but it's all over in less than a minute.

I'VE ONLY JUST MANAGED to pull up my pants when Annie walks back into the bar. I turn away so she won't see the liquid desire shimmering in my eyes, or the short gasps I draw in for breath. Blake, however, is utterly relaxed. He barely glances at her over his shoulder and not by a flicker does he betray that anything is amiss, even though I know that beneath the hem of his shirt, hidden from view, his pants are still undone.

"The room's ready!" Annie announces, then, catching sight of the empty glass, "oh, you poured yourself a drink." She's not sure whether to be relieved or annoyed.

"I did," Blake says. "A scotch – the Balcones. You can bill it to our room."

"I'll do that. Would you like another?" She includes me in the offer, but all I can do is shake my head. I'm still trying to catch my breath, while Blake stands there, cool as a cucumber.

"Not right now," he says. "We've been on the road all day, I think we'll just get cleaned up. Do you know if there's anywhere nearby we can get something to eat?"

"Oh, *Café Gitana* is just down the road, you can't miss it. It's not even a five-minute walk."

Blake looks at me, senses I'm bushed, and speaks again. "On second thoughts, any good takeout places? We can try the café tomorrow."

"There's a *Domino's* in town. I'm sure you can order online, and I'll let you know when it's here."

"Great, thanks, Annie." He picks up our discarded bags. "Shall we?" he asks, cocking his head in my direction. I stifle a nervous giggle and follow him out, as Annie leads us up the stairs to our room.

"That was insane," I say, once the sound of Annie's footfalls on the stairs has died away. Blake has dumped our bags by the door and he's leaning against it, watching me closely. Under such intense scrutiny, I find myself feeling inexplicably shy about what just happened.

"Why didn't you tell me?"

I open my arms helplessly. "It's not exactly the kind of thing you tell people."

"I'm not people, Cat."

"I know. I wanted to tell you, but I was scared it might freak you out."

"Freak me out? To find out that my girlfriend has an incredibly high sex drive? That she's not shy to try new things? Are you even listening to yourself? Shit, I feel like I just won the Lasker. It's an award," he adds, catching sight of my confusion. He comes over to sit next to me on the bed and takes both of my hands in his. "The point is, this isn't exactly a bad thing. Not from my perspective, anyway."

"You don't think that I'm some depraved, physical creature who's just using you for sex?" I tease.

"I think you're the woman I fell in love with. An incredible woman. And I have zero problem with you using me for sex, so long as you love me, too. Just so we're clear." He gives me a look that tells me he wouldn't mind me using him again, right now, and I grin.

"I should've told you ages ago."

"You should've," he agrees. "But I'm not surprised you didn't. I blame society – he's a hero, she's a whore, and all that." He stops, and his face turns somber.

"What is it?" I ask, terrified he's changed his mind.

"Your ex," he murmurs, "you and him used to do things like this? Like what we did downstairs?"

Oh shit. "I don't want to"

"But you have to," he interrupts. "No more secrets, Cat. I need to know what I'm up against."

I take a steadying breath. "Yes. We used to do things like that."

"You ever try with anyone else?"

"Not until now."

He squeezes my hand. "Is that why you were so hung up on him?"

I bob my head, trying to swallow the pain and guilt building into a hard lump in my throat.

"I told you, I didn't think anyone would understand."

"You were wrong. I know you don't believe that yet, so I guess it's up to me to prove it to you." He gets to his feet and offers me his hand. "I want to make one thing very clear, though, Catrina. I love you for who you are, for the real you, the person in here." He lays his hand over my heart. "This other stuff," he adds, a twinkle in his eye, "that's just an added bonus."

He leads me to the shower, where he proceeds to wash me gently from head to toe, kneading away the tension in my body with strong, supple fingers. He massages shampoo into my scalp and then uses almost half a bottle of conditioner to comb through my hair. It's almost more intimate than sex, but not once does he try anything more. Goose flesh rises on my arms whenever his fingers skim near my breasts, or over my thighs.

When I finally step out of the cubicle, dripping water all over the floor, I feel cleaner than I've ever felt in my life. It's as if Blake has washed all the ugliness I've been holding onto, away.

He orders two large pizzas, and pays online. Alice brings them up, with a firm warning that boxes are to be disposed of. We eat. We talk. We cuddle. I fall asleep in his arms, feeling safe, and loved, and wondering how I was ever stupid enough to risk losing him.

We sleep in on Saturday morning and almost miss breakfast. Two other couples are staying at the *Step Right Inn,* a pair of newlyweds, a few years younger than I am, and one older couple, whose youngest child recently went off to college and who are finally fulfilling their lifelong ambition to visit all fifty states. The younger couple keeps to themselves, cocooned in newly married bliss, but David and Mandy Friedman, the intrepid travelers, seem intent on making new friends along the way. Blake referred to me as his girlfriend when we introduced ourselves, which made me ridiculously happy.

"Where are you folks from?" David asks, once he's given us a play-by-play of their travels.

"Oakland," Blake replies, "Cat's born and bred, but I'm originally from Sacramento. I'm completing my residency. It's my last year, actually."

"Will you stay in Oakland, once you're done?" Mandy asks the question, and it occurs to me that I don't know the answer. Blake has never mentioned anything beyond the end of this final year. I lean forward, as eager for his reply as the Friedmans.

"At this stage, I'm not sure where I'll end up. I've sent out applications to a number of hospitals across the country. I guess it just depends on who offers me a job."

The conversation continues, but I've tuned out. If Blake gets offered a job somewhere else, what does that mean for us?

"YOU'RE AWFULLY QUIET," Blake says as we head out to do some sightseeing. The B&B is comfortable enough, but there's not much to do. Blake has booked a day tour of Universal Studios for tomorrow, but today I'm content to walk along the beach, feeling the sand in my toes and listening to the roaring hiss of the waves breaking against the shore.

I offer him a shy smile. "I'm still trying to process everything that's happened."

He only nods, and slips his hand through mine. It's a small gesture, but it's comforting. Being like this with Blake, open and honest, is like taking off a pair of too-tight shoes after a miserable day.

We pass an ice-cream stand, and Blake gets us each a double-scooped cone, which we eat on the beach, sharing sweet, vanilla kisses and watching the sea, until the sky darkens and ominous thunderheads roll in. Blake gets to his feet before helping me up. We only just make it to a small, seaside diner before the heavens open.

"What can I get you?" The bored-looking waitress asks.

"Two coffees, please," Blake replies, then grins at me as she saunters off to place the order. The coffee is tepid, and the ladies room, when I go to use it, is filthy, but nothing seems to bother me, Nothing can penetrate the cocoon of happiness I'm insulated in. Not even a text message from Aaron, which comes through while Blake is paying the bill, which I delete without reading.

"You sure you're okay?" Blake asks when I get back to the table. "You've been awfully quiet today."

"Actually, I've been thinking about what you said to the Friedmans. About possibly moving when your residency is up."

"Ah," he says knowingly. "I'm sorry, I should've thought that through before I said it."

"What happens if you get a position across the country?"

"Well, that, I have been thinking about. I know your business is taking off, but most of your work is done online, right? And via email?"

"Yes," I draw out the word, sensing where this is headed. "But that doesn't mean I can just pick up and move. What about my apartment? My mom? My whole life is in Oakland."

"Your whole life was in Oakland," he corrects. "When you were with Aaron. No, hear me out," he continues, as my mouth tightens at the mention of Aaron's name. "Your business is moveable, your apartment would be easy to let out. Your mom, I can understand, but to be honest, I think you should focus on yourself. Cat, you're getting divorced. You deserve a fresh start."

The concern that has been building in my chest evaporates when I realize that Blake is not expecting me to uproot my life just because he says so. He wants me to move for me, so that I can truly move on, without the burden of my past.

"If you don't want to move, we will still make this work," he says, with fierce determination. "I'm not losing you. We'll find a way, even if I have to apply to every hospital on the West Coast and sleep on airplanes for the rest of my life."

"You would do that?"

When he smiles at me like that, I would follow him anywhere. "What part of I love you did you not understand?"

"But we've only been together six months. You've wanted to be a surgeon your whole life. I would never ask you to compromise your job for me."

"You're not asking me to. It's called working together," he teases. "We'll find a solution, Cat. Call me crazy, but I'd like to think I can have the job, *and* the girl."

Aaron and I may have been together for five years, but I'd never felt like we were a team. Aaron is selfish by nature, and I'd been too wrapped up in my own issues, anyway. Blake, on the other hand, makes me feel like, together, we could take on the whole world and live to tell the tale.

12

"I'm going to be sick," I say on Monday morning as Blake and I stand before the revolving glass doors that lead into the Bennett Communications building. Never mind the whole world, right now I can't seem to summon the courage to face one man. The bliss of the past two days made it easy to forget the real reason that we're here.

"No, you're not," Blake says firmly. "Just breathe."

We'd called ahead to check that Stephen Bennett would be in the office today, but standing here, knowing that my father is somewhere beyond these doors, is both overwhelming and terrifying.

Blake gives me only a few seconds before he turns to face me. "You ready?"

"No."

He takes my hand. "Let's go."

I trail behind him, clinging to his hand like a lifeline, and we enter the building together, the revolving doors spitting us out into a classy foyer. Behind the stretch of oak which serves as a reception counter, a middle-aged woman in a black silk shirt gazes up at us.

"May I help you?" she asks politely.

"Stephen Bennett," Blake says brusquely. "Is he here?"

"Do you have an appointment?" She scans her computer screen, a small frown creasing her brow.

"It's a private matter."

"I'm afraid Mr. Bennett has back-to-back meetings this morning. I'd be happy to let him know you popped by"

"I'm sorry, but it really is imperative that we see him," Blake cuts across her gentle dismissal. "Would you tell him that a friend of Viola Davis is here to see him."

Her lips purse. This is not a woman who likes to be told what to do, and particularly on her own turf.

"I really think it would be best if"

"Not to be rude, Ma'am, but your opinion on what's best is not relevant right now. Please could you get Mr. Bennett on the phone. As I said, it's important." Blake's natural self-assertiveness beats her back. Bristling, she lifts the telephone on her desk and dials an extension, all the while casting dark looks at Blake which make her feelings plain. I don't care. My legs have started to tremble, and I think I'm about to hyperventilate. I peek over my shoulder at the doors, wondering if I should make a run for it.

"Breathe," Blake murmurs, reading my thoughts.

After a quick conversation, the receptionist replaces the handset and gets to her feet.

"Mr. Bennett has asked that you take a seat in the boardroom," she says. She can't seem to bring herself to be friendly, even though her boss has obviously deemed us worthy of his time. She leaves us in the vast room, closing the door behind her with a firm click.

"Do you think he's nervous?" I ask Blake. I'm too highly-strung to sit, so I pace the length of the polished oak table.

"Probably. He's married, and no one wants to be reminded of their old flame, especially at work."

"Do you think I should've called first?"

He considers this a moment and then shakes his head. "No. This isn't something you tell someone over the phone. Breathe, Cat. I'm here. I'll be with you the whole time."

I walk the length of the table again, wringing my hands together so tightly they ache.

"I have no idea what I'm going to say to him."

Blake steps in front of me. "You're going to wear down that carpet," he teases, steering me toward one of twelve identical chairs. "Sit."

I do as I'm told, and when he's satisfied that I'm not going to leap up and start pacing again, he busies himself with the coffee machine in the corner of the room.

I take a sip from the cup he offers me and almost spit it out. It's revoltingly sweet.

"You need the sugar," Blake says.

"It's disgusting."

"Drink it. Doctor's orders."

I almost drop the cup when the doors open, and Stephen Bennett walks into the room. He is tall, not as tall as Blake, but somehow more imposing, and he has the air of a man who knows he's vitally important. His hair is dark, so different from my natural red, and silvering at the temples, but his eyes, when they scan the room to rest on me, are the exact hazel of my own. The second they land on me, he gives a visible start, he looks as if he's seen a ghost.

Realizing that fear has struck me dumb, Blake steps forward to extend his hand.

"Mr. Bennett, my name is Blake Stanton. This," he adds, releasing Stephen's hand and gesturing toward me, "is Catrina Davis."

Stephen Bennett's face darkens at the mention of my last name. To be fair, my name now is actually Catrina James, but for the purpose of this exercise, using my maiden name is a smart move.

"You're Viola's daughter?" he asks. It's a fair guess, given that my mother is an only child.

"Yes." I stumble to my feet and extend my hand. Stephen ignores it. Out of the corner of my eye, I see Blake stiffen. "I'm sorry to barge in on you like this, Mr. Bennett. I'm sure you must very busy"

"I am," he snaps, cutting me off. "And no disrespect, Miss Davis, but your mother isn't someone I would consider a friend, so I'm not quite sure what it is you're doing here."

My hand is still outstretched. I snatch it back.

"From what I hear, you were friends, at one time."

He recoils. Darts a glance in Blake's direction and finds only steely resolve there.

"What do you want?"

I breathe in, filling my lungs to bursting. "Mr. Bennett, I think..." I lose my nerve, but Blake steps closer and rests his hand on the small of my back. "I think I'm your daughter," I finish, quietly.

Stephen's response is almost comical. He frowns, then starts to smile, as if he might laugh. He doesn't. Instead, the slight upward tilt of his lips plummets into a furious scowl.

"Is this some kind of joke?" But even as he says it, he's scanning my face. Finding the similarities that lie there – the eyes, the shape of my lips, the point of my chin.

"No," Blake says. "It's not a joke. And I know this must come as a shock, but we've traveled a long way to see you. Catrina only just discovered your identity, and she'd obviously like to find out more about you. I'm sure you also have questions of your own."

"Only one," Stephen corrects. His eyes bore into me, but I have no idea what he's thinking because his face gives nothing away. When he speaks, however, there's no mistaking the venom in his voice. "Who the hell put you up to this?"

HE DOESN'T BELIEVE ME. My father thinks that I'm a fraud. Whether or not he thinks I want money, I can't be sure, because he doesn't directly come out and say it, but I suspect that's exactly what he believes. I can't do anything but swallow down the humiliation as he hurls his outrage toward me, wave after wave of accusatory vitriol.

It doesn't take long for Blake to intervene.

"Enough!" he roars, taking in the tears shimmering in my eyes and the way I'm cowering away from Stephen. "Leave her alone, you son of a bitch! I swear to God, if you don't shut your mouth, I'll do it for you. Can't you see what you're doing to her?"

"What *I'm* doing to *her*?" Stephen sneers. "She arrives here, unannounced, and starts making ludicrous claims, and I'm supposed to feel guilty? I don't know what you people are playing at, but I'm not buying it."

Blake steps right into Stephen's face. "She. Is. Not. People," he growls, slow and menacing, "She is your God-damned blood, you miserable bastard. And you don't deserve her." He raises his hand, and for a second, I think he's going to hit Stephen, but instead, he draws his wallet from his pocket and hands him a card. "Here are my contact details. If you come to your senses and decide to become a decent human being, get in touch. And if Catrina still wants to talk to you, you might just stand a chance of getting to know your daughter. Not that you deserve her," he adds ominously. Then, he offers me his hand. "Come on, baby. Let's get out of here."

WE DON'T SPEAK as Blake leads me outside, his hand clutching mine so tightly that it starts to tingle with lack of blood flow. I barely care. Meek and mute, I follow him, putting one foot in front of the other. Seeing my distress, the receptionist allows herself a small smirk. The second I'm inside the safety of the pick-up and Blake closes the door behind me, I burst into tears. Chest-heaving, bone-breaking sobs, which wrack my body and claw their way up my throat. Blake doesn't console me. Not here, in front of this awful building, in full view of anyone who might choose to look out of a window. Only when we've driven a few blocks, does he pull into a parking lot and haul me into his arms. For a long time, he holds me, until my tears run dry and the ache in my heart hardens, giving way to a quiet fury.

"He doesn't deserve you," Blake murmurs into my hair. He's trying to convince me, but when I test my shattered pride, I find no convincing necessary.

"I know."

Blake raises his head, a small frown creasing between his eyes. This isn't the reaction he was expecting.

I draw in a shaky breath, the remnants of my emotional breakdown wreaking havoc on my breathing. "I'm not stupid. I know I haven't done anything wrong. I know he could've handled that better. I also know that he's probably a world class prick." I wipe the last of the tears from my cheeks and attempt a tentative smile. "But at least now I know."

Blake puts his hand on my leg and gives it a squeeze. "I'm proud of you."

"Thanks for being here. I don't think I could've handled that alone."

He kisses me, and then puts the pick-up into drive.

"Where are we going?" I ask as we pull out of the parking lot.

"Home," Blake replies simply.

13

We drive six hours straight. Emotionally exhausted, I doze on and off for the last three. I'd tried valiantly to stay awake, to keep Blake company, but eventually, he'd balled up his jacket, shoved it up against my window as a makeshift pillow, and ordered me to sleep.

He wakes me as we approach my apartment block, with a gentle hand on my shoulder. "Good afternoon, beautiful."

I blink the sleep out of my eyes and clear my throat. "We're home already?"

"And not a minute too soon. I don't think I could've taken one more second of your snoring."

"I do not snore!"

"You're right. What you do sounds more like sawing through bone, by hand." He winks at me as he pulls into the underground lot and takes his usual parking space beside my car.

We're both laughing as we get out and stretch our cramped legs. The smiles play about our lips as we cast knowing glances at one another during the elevator ride. I survived. I went through something awful, but I survived. I'm not broken, and we're okay. I brush my hand across the nape of Blake's neck, and then step forward to kiss him, full on the mouth. His lips curve against mine in a knowing smile.

"You seem to be feeling better," he whispers against my lips.

"I know something that will make me feel a lot better," I reply coyly, lowering my hand to grab a fistful of denim-clad backside. Blake laughs, but he mirrors my action.

The elevator doors open and we pull apart. The light, teasing atmosphere vanishes, the second I step out into the hall to find my mother crouched on my doorstep.

"MOM?"

Her head jerks up at the sound of my voice. Her eyes are glittering, never a good sign, and her make-up which, by the heaviness of it, must have been on since last night, is streaked down her face.

"Cat!" she practically yells. "How dare you? How *dare* you!"

There's no doubt in my mind that she knows where I've been and who I've spoken to. Or that she's high as a kite. *Fine, we'll do this now*, I think furiously. I keep my voice flat and tell her to come inside.

"Don't tell me what to do!" she yells back, with all the manic fury of a two-year-old denied a delicate family heirloom.

"Keep your voice down, mom," I hiss, frantically trying to jab my key into the lock. "I have neighbors."

"I don't give a damn about your neighbors!" She turns her head to yell the last words at the apartment door across from mine.

"Inside!" I hiss.

Blake follows us in and then plants himself at the edge of my living room, ready to intervene if he needs to. My mother trips over the couch on her way in, and he catches her arm, keeping her upright. She doesn't even thank him.

"I need you to go," I tell him gently. I appreciate what he's doing, but this is not something I want him to witness. Bad enough that he's seen what happened with Stephen, I don't need him up front and center for the Broadway musical that my mother's about to perform.

"I'm not leaving you."

"Please." I put a hand on his arm. "I need to do this alone." My eyes tell him what my lips cannot – that I'm ashamed – and his expression softens.

"I'll wait in the bedroom," he concedes, "but I'm not leaving this apartment."

"Fair enough."

Without another word, he walks down the hall and leaves me alone with my mother.

"How could you do this to me, Catrina?" she repeats, the second she has my attention.

"Do what to you, mom? I haven't done anything *to* you. This hasn't even got anything to do with you!"

"It's got everything to do with me! How do you think I felt, getting a call from *that* man, after all these years?"

"I'm surprised you even knew who *that* man was, given the state you're in. Don't you dare!" I add, snatching away the joint she's pulled from her bag. "You've had enough." Proving my point, she sways on her feet. "Sit down before you fall over and break something."

"You don't get to speak to me like that. You may not like it, but I'm your mother."

"You want me to speak to you with respect?" I taunt, "then earn it. You're so far gone you can barely stand."

"Barely stand the sight of you, you mean, after what you've done," she slurs, then looks absurdly pleased with herself for being so clever as to come up with it. I know that she's vicious when she's high, but it still hurts.

"Jesus, mom, this is serious. For once in my life, I'd just like to have a normal conversation with you about something that matters. I met my father today! I know it's not what you wanted, but it's what I needed. And he treated me like *shit*." My voice breaks, and I slump onto the couch. My mother hesitates.

"He what?" she blinks, rapidly, as if trying to clear the drug-induced fog from her brain. "What did he do to you, Cat?"

"He all but kicked me out. He didn't believe me." Fresh waves of humiliation redden my cheeks. "He called me a liar."

"That lousy, rotten son of a bitch! I'll rip his throat out with my bare hands! How dare he"

"Mom! Enough! Please." I close my eyes to shut out the sound of her ranting. She falls silent and a moment later I feel the couch dip beside me under her weight.

"Cat?" she asks, in a voice much smaller than I expect. I turn my face to peer up at her with one eye.

"I need you to go, mom."

"Go?" It's as if I just asked her what the square root of pi is.

"Yes, mom. Just go."

"No."

"No?" It's my turn to be outraged.

"No," she repeats. "I'm not leaving. I know that you're upset, but you don't get to turn this around. None of this would have happened if you hadn't gone behind my back."

"I beg your pardon?" I can't believe what I'm hearing. I'd believed, for a nano-second, that she felt sorry for me. That she would comfort me – her daughter – after everything that I'd been through. I should have known better. Viola Davis has only ever cared about Viola Davis.

"I told you to leave it alone, didn't I?" she says, oblivious to the warning look I throw her. "Now look what you've done. That bastard kicked you out, like you were nothing, and he threatened to sue me for about a dozen things that I don't even understand."

"Let me get this straight," I say, speaking slowly and clearly. "You're saying that this is all my fault? That you're an innocent victim?"

"Well, I wouldn't say it in that many words, but there's no doubt that you brought this upon both of us. You've never listened to me, Cat. Maybe now you'll realize that sometimes I actually do know what's best for you."

"Ha!" I bark, my laughter raw and raging. "You know what's best for me, do you?" I launch to my feet and pull down the ladder to the attic. "Tell me, mom, was growing up without a father, or any knowledge of who he was, good for me? Was missing six weeks of my senior year, and failing chemistry, all because you decided we should road trip around the States, good for me? Was getting taken to the emergency room because you spiked my tea, good for me? Was being two hours late for *my own fucking wedding* because you were passed out in the bathroom good for me?" While I'm shrieking, I've ascended the steps and am fumbling around in the dark with my hands. My fingers brush against the edge of a canvas, and I haul it out with a triumphant cry. "Is this good for me, mom?" I say, tossing it down to the ground, where it clatters near her feet. Another painting follows, then another, then another, until I feel strong hands grip my waist.

"Enough, Cat," Blake says, his voice infinitely kind. I whirl to find him standing behind me, his tired eyes reproachful as he shakes his head. "Enough, sweetheart," he whispers. With abject horror, my eyes move past him to find my mother standing amidst a mountain of her own work, her hand pressed to her mouth, her eyes filled with tears. *Oh, God. Oh, God, what have I done?*

BLAKE DRIVES MY MOTHER HOME. We hadn't spoken a word to each other after he carried me off the ladder, past the maelstrom of my living room, and into my room. He'd laid me on the bed, kissed me on the forehead, and promised he'd be right back. I hadn't been able to move, curled on my side, filled with remorse so powerful it edged my vision black. I'd heard him speaking, coaxing my silent mother through the jumble of canvases and out of the front door, and then I'd heard nothing but my own thudding heartbeat, echoing in my ears.

I wake up to find Blake in bed beside me, snoring softly, his tanned arm slung over my waist. The memory of everything that happened yesterday hits me like a ton of bricks, and I close my eyes, willing back the oblivion of sleep. Instead, my brain goes into hyperdrive, replaying every awful moment until I slip from the bed and immerse myself under a scalding hot shower.

It's not minutes before Blake's blurred silhouette appears before the frosted glass. He's wearing a pair of tracksuit pants, and nothing else. When he opens the door, his eyes pose a silent question.

"Hi," I say.

"Hi. How are you feeling?"

"Awful."

"I thought you might. Here, give me that." He takes the sponge from my hands and lathers it with soap, as efficiently and thoroughly as if he were prepping for surgery. "You can't blame yourself, Cat," he murmurs, twirling his finger to indicate that I should turn around. I do, and he starts to wash my back.

"I was so cruel to her," I mumble. It's easier to admit now that I don't have to look at him, and I wonder if that's exactly what he intended.

"Yes, but I think you were justified. I heard what she said to you. She was awful first."

"She's not in her right mind," I say as he drops the sponge and starts to knead the tension out of my shoulders with his strong hands. "It's like being cruel to a badly behaved child."

"You make too many excuses for her. We spoke a little, on the way back to her place. She's not as naïve as she'd like you to believe."

I whirl to face him. "What did she say to you?"

"Nothing that would make you feel better. I'm sorry."

"*I'm* sorry. After everything I've put you through, and now having to deal with this mess... it's a wonder you're still here."

He gives me a small smile. "I wouldn't want to be anywhere else, love. Together, remember? We handle it together – the good, and the bad."

I allow myself a moment to forget the horror of yesterday, to forget everything but right here and right now. I lean out of the shower, uncaring of the water streaming onto the floor, and curl my right hand around his neck, drawing him toward me, until he gets the idea. Without dropping his pants, he steps into the cubicle and takes me in his arms. When we kiss, water streams into my mouth, until Blake closes his lips over mine, and then it's just the warmth of his hot mouth on mine, and our breath rising in the steam.

"WHAT DO you think I should do?" I ask Blake later. We're in the kitchen, armed with coffee. The smell of toast still lingers in the air.

"Nothing," Blake replies.

"I can't do nothing. I can't leave things like this."

"You can, for now. You've said your piece, Cat. Maybe not in the most constructive way, but your point needed to be made. Let her stew for a bit. She needs to know you're serious."

He's right. The more I think about it, and even though I'm still cringing at the way I dealt with my mother, it needed to happen. I am tired of caving. I'm tired of being the person who tries, and fails, because the people in my life couldn't give a damn. My mother, Aaron – it's an endless cycle. From now on, things are going to be different, I vow to myself as I kiss Blake goodbye.

"I wish I didn't have to go," he says. "I feel bad leaving you."

"You have work to do," I tell him. "Hell, I have work to do." We'd taken the last three days for ourselves, but the world waits for no one. Life carries on, even when you feel like it's falling apart. Blake has his internship, and I have my business, and both require us to show up.

"Are you going to work down at the coffee shop this morning?"

"Probably. Routine is good in times of trauma, or so I've heard."

He chuckles. "Look at you, getting back on the horse."

I grin up at him. "I have an excellent instructor."

As he leans in for another kiss, his phone rings, He rolls his eyes and pulls it from his pocket, then peers at the screen in confusion.

"Hello?"

I hear a male voice, but I can't make out what he's saying. Blake has gone deadly still. "Yes, Stephen, what can I do for you?"

He listens for a second. "Well, that would be up to Catrina." *He wants to see you,* he tells me. I snatch up my bottom lip between my teeth, considering. Blake comes to a decision. "Let me speak to her. I'll let you know what she decides." Without waiting for an answer, he hangs up.

"What was that about?" I ask.

"He's coming here."

"Here?"

"To Oakland. He wants to take us for dinner – or, rather, take *you* for dinner, tomorrow night."

"Twenty-four hours ago he was throwing me out, and now he wants to take me for dinner?"

Blake smiles. "Is everything out of your mouth going to be a question?"

"Maybe."

"For what it's worth, I think you should go. Yesterday didn't go well, and if you never want to see him again, I'm more than happy to tell him that, but I think you should hear him out. For you," he adds, meaningfully, "not for him."

I nod. "Tell him yes."

THE DIVORCE ATTORNEY had promised that Aaron would be served within five working days. They were a day late. On Wednesday morning, just a few minutes after Blake has left for the hospital, I hear a knock at the door. Caught by surprise, I open it to find Aaron in the doorway, his hair uncharacteristically mussed up, as if he's been running his hands through it all morning. He's holding a sheaf of papers.

"Aaron! What are you doing here?" It's been a little over a week since I last saw him, but he looks awful.

He shoulders his way past me. I grit my teeth and shut the door.

"What the fuck is this?" he asks, hurling the papers at me. They land in a heap at my feet.

"You know exactly what it is."

"A divorce, Cat? You're filing for a divorce?"

Calmly, I retrieve the papers. "It's what people do when they no longer want to be married."

"We both know you don't want to divorce me."

"Actually, I do." To my surprise, he's shaking with emotion. "Come on, Aaron. You don't want to be married to me, either. Why drag this out any longer?"

"It's this new man, isn't it? The doctor? I saw him leave this morning. You got back together with him, didn't you?" he says it as if I've committed a cardinal sin, which is ironic considering he only really wants me when I'm unavailable. "He's put you up to this."

"Are you serious?" my eyes widen with disbelief. "We've been separated for over a year, Aaron! I should've done this twelve months ago, when I found you screwing Staci on our couch!"

"Don't try to turn this on her. You love that I'm with Staci! You've been lusting after me like a bitch on heat since she and I hooked up. She's the best thing that ever happened to us!"

I am at a complete and utter loss for words. "You've lost your mind."

His expression changes, something dark and feral glinting in his eyes.

"Oh really?" he takes a predatory step closer. "Then explain this." He pulls a scrap of lace from his pocket. It's the underwear I was wearing that morning at Verdure. It feels like a lifetime ago, but I still cringe at the sight. "Admit it, Cat, you want me. God knows the sex has never been better. And it was good before, but now..." I stand, mortified, as he brings his hand to his face and inhales deeply. "You don't want to give this up," Aaron croaks thickly. I feel it then – the traitorous tug deep inside of me, the twisted part of me that wants him as badly as he wants me. I draw up a mental image of Blake and brandish it like a shield in my mind.

"I don't want this," I say firmly. "I am *happy*, Aaron. Happier than I ever was with you. Our relationship was toxic, it held us both back from finding something real. You have to know that. Please, just let me go."

Aaron steps closer until we're almost touching. I ball my hands into fists.

"Don't do this, Kitty Cat."

"I won't be your bit on the side, Aaron. Not anymore."

"You want me to leave Staci? Done."

"You're lying."

His hand cups my chin, forcing my face upward. "I am not losing you," he growls. His eyes dip to my chest, where I can feel my nipples pressing through the soft cotton of my nightshirt. His lazy grin infuriates me. I may be strong enough to stand against him, but my traitorous body hasn't caught up yet.

"Who do you think you're fooling, Cat?" he asks.

"Get out."

His long fingers caress the underside of my chin. "Do you remember Verdure?" The heat rises in my cheeks as he raises the hand still holding my ruined panties. "This keepsake reminds me, Cat. It reminds me how I fucked you up against that door while your boyfriend sat just a few feet away. That was only a few weeks ago. You expect me to believe you've had a complete change of heart in just a few weeks?"

The mention of Blake snaps me back to reality. "Get out of my house!" I turn toward the door, intent on forcing him to go, when I stop dead. Blake is standing in the open doorway, his chalk-white face a mask of bleak disgust. He's still holding his key – the one I gave him as a symbol of my commitment. I hadn't even heard him come in. It takes me only a second to realize that Aaron would have seen him enter because he's facing the door.

"Blake!" I stumble over my words. "When did you—"

"A while ago." His voice is curt, clipped, not a trace of warmth in his brown eyes as they slide toward Aaron. "I guess you must be the ex-husband."

Aaron words are flippant. "Husband," he corrects, tapping the papers in my hands. "Nothing ex about it."

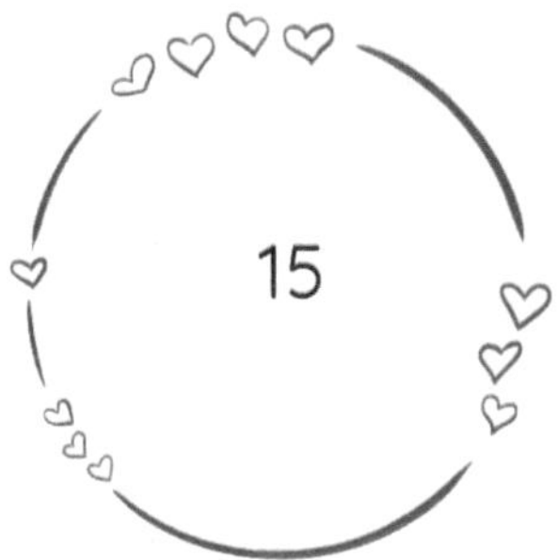

I chase Blake into the hall, leaving Aaron alone in my apartment.

"You have to let me explain!" I sob, stumbling into the elevator after him.

"Explain what?" Blake roars, angrier than I've ever seen him. "Explain how you've been screwing that prick the whole time we've been dating?"

"It's not like that!"

"Oh, really? Then what is it like, Cat? Because from what I just heard, it's exactly like that."

"He said that because he knew you were listening!"

"You're saying it *didn't* happen like that?"

"I'm saying I ended it! I signed the papers! I told you, I don't want to be that person anymore."

"So you finally ended it, after months of cheating on me, and I'm supposed to be impressed? Jesus, Cat, I knew you had issues, but you're something else."

"I didn't plan any of this. I swear, I wasn't seeing him when we met. We bumped into each other a few months ago and it just happened."

"It just happened?" he gives a harsh bark of laughter. "I'm a surgeon, Cat. I have a pretty sound knowledge of the human anatomy, and believe me, it doesn't just happen." He claps his hand to his forehead, covering his eyes, and then drags it down his face. "Verdure, Cat?" The disgust and pain in his voice breaks my heart.

"I'm sorry," I whisper. "I'm so, so sorry. I can explain everything. If you just come back in, we could talk about it"

"I'm not interested. I have *nothing* to say to you."

The elevator reaches the ground floor and the doors open. "Please..."

Blake shakes his head. Unshed tears shimmer in his eyes. "You screwed him while I ordered your eggs. What kind of person does that?"

I don't answer, because the question is rhetorical. We both know the kind of person who does that. A monster.

AARON IS LOUNGING on my couch when I return. Just the sight of him makes me sick to my stomach.

"You need to leave," I snap. I hold the door open to emphasize my urgency.

"Why? Things are just starting to get interesting." He's lost all trace of the desperate man who walked into my apartment. Instead, there's a swagger in his tone. He's amused, I think with disgust. And thrilled with the unexpected turn of events.

I snatch up the papers, which I'd dumped on the table in the hall on my mad dash after Blake.

"Sign them."

Aaron rises from the couch. "I don't think I will."

"You know that I can divorce you, with or without your signature on these papers, right? And I will. All you're doing is delaying the inevitable."

"No, baby. *You're* delaying the inevitable." He comes to stand right before me, and with one lazy flick of his wrist, knocks the papers out of my hands. "You can't fight this, Kitty Cat. Try all you like, but I guarantee we will be seeing each other real soon." His eyes dip to my chest, still heaving with emotion, and his gaze lingers there. "I, for one, am looking forward to it."

I GET NO WORK DONE. After Aaron left, I'd come down to the coffee shop as planned, but I shouldn't have bothered. My vision keeps blurring as unbidden tears slip over my eyelids and track their way down my cheeks. Amy checks on me at first, but after a while she seems to realize I just want to be left alone and goes back to refilling my cup every hour, on the hour, while I stare, unseeing, at a blank screen. I text Blake, telling him again how sorry I am, but hear nothing back. Instead, I receive a message from Stephen Bennett, confirming the time and place of our dinner tonight. Blake must have given him my number, and the thought that he'd done that – that he'd removed himself from this situation with my father, crucifies me. At two o'clock I send him another text message, and then I pay my bill and head home. My apartment feels empty without him in it. My heart feels the same. I lie on my bed with only my dark thoughts for company and try to figure out a way to move past this. There's nothing I can do about Blake. I can't blame him for walking out on me. What I did was unforgivable. But my mother, and Stephen Bennett, I can do something about. Blake may be gone, but I still have the lessons he taught me. To put myself first. To be selfish, if I need to. To speak my truth. And I plan to do all of it.

STEPHEN IS ALREADY SEATED at the table when I arrive. He's staying at the Marriott, but we meet at a restaurant a few blocks away. It's Italian, the walls adorned with chalk paintings of wine bottles, famous landmarks, and fresh tomatoes. Beaded chandeliers hang from the ceilings and the chairs are covered in crushed red velvet. Stephen stands when I reach the table.

"Catrina," he says, by way of greeting. He's outwardly calm, but I can tell by the way his fingers tremble when he gestures toward my seat, that he's not as composed as he'd like to make out. "Thank you for coming."

"I almost didn't," I admit.

"After what happened on Monday, I wouldn't have blamed you. What changed your mind?"

"Blake." It's a simple, honest answer.

"I'll be sure to thank him when I see him next."

I don't think that will ever happen, but I stay silent. I don't want to talk about Blake. It sends a sharp, shooting pain through my chest every time I think of him. Unfortunately, Stephen's next words don't help my cause.

"Will he be joining us this evening?" he asks.

"No." My answer is clipped, I realize, as I say it. "I'm sorry, I don't really want to talk about Blake. We had a fight, and to be honest, I don't actually know where things stand between us right now. It was my fault," I add quickly.

"I'm sorry to hear that," he says, and he sounds sincere. "I hope you manage to work things out. He seems like a good man."

There's an awkward silence as Stephen tries to look encouraging while I fight the urge to burst into tears.

"I wanted to apologize," he says eventually. "For how I behaved. I know it won't excuse the way I treated you, but I am truly sorry for everything I said. And for implying that you were lying."

"You believe me now?" I can't help but wonder what changed his mind so drastically in just twenty-four hours.

He sighs, his fingers toying with the napkin on the table before him. "I knew you were telling the truth the second I walked through the door."

"How?"

A ghost of a smile. "You... you have a sister, Catrina. Her name is Hannah, and she looks just like you." When Stephen had first seen me, he'd balked, as if he'd seen a ghost. Somewhere in my addled brain, this now makes sense, but I'm too stunned to pay attention.

"I have a sister?"

"You do. She's only sixteen."

"Oh my God." I sit back in my chair. I'd never even considered the possibility that I might have siblings. "Oh my God. Can I..." I trail off, realizing that I have no idea whether he's even prepared to tell his family about me. "Do you think I might get to meet her one day?"

"I think she'd like that. Actually," he laughs, low and deep, "she's already told me that if I don't bring her out by next weekend, she's going to steal my car and drive out here herself. And if you ever saw Hannah behind the wheel, you'd know that's a very bad idea."

I'm still reeling, and I don't even register his attempt to lighten the atmosphere. "You told her about me?"

"I did. You're her sister, how could I not? My wife, Lucy, would like to meet you too."

He told his *wife* about me? My surprise must show on my face because Stephen laughs.

"Like I said, we got off on the wrong foot. I know how it must have looked, but I promise I'm not a bad guy. You caught me off guard, and I reacted without thinking. I'll never be able to tell you how sorry I am for that."

"This is a good start," I admit. "I never would have expected you to tell your family about me, especially so soon."

"They're your family too, Catrina," he says. Something warm and beautiful blossoms in my chest. "If you're up to it, I'd like to fly back with them next weekend. I have to leave tomorrow. I wish I could've stayed longer, but I left rather abruptly, and I have commitments at work that I can't get out of at such short notice."

"Next weekend is perfect, or whenever it suits you. Please don't feel you have to upheave your whole life just for me."

"It's hard not to want to," he says. "I have so much time to make up for." He takes a sip of his scotch and shakes his head. "This is so surreal. To think I have a daughter your age, it's going to take some getting used to. I don't know if your grandparents or your mother told you, but I'm only"

"Forty," I finish for him. "I heard. And believe me, it's as weird for me as it is for you." We both pause in embarrassment as we work out that, to the other diners, we are as likely to look like lovers as father and daughter. Stephen clears his throat.

"I should also tell you that I contacted your mother. Shortly after you left my office."

"I heard about that too."

"I wasn't very kind to her either," he admits. "But I'd be lying if I said I'm not furious with her." His fingers drum the table. "She should have told me," he mutters. "I had a right to know that I had fathered a child."

"I know. We both deserved the truth, but my mother wasn't the only one at fault in that regard."

A flash of real anger crosses his face. "She told me. If my parents were still alive, I'd at least be able to take my anger out on someone else. Sadly, your mother was the only available target."

It still feels so strange to hear of family I never knew existed, but I can't say I'm particularly sorry to hear that his parents are deceased. From what little I know of them, I doubt we would have gotten along. Still, they were his parents, so I try to invoke a shred of empathy as I ask, "what happened to them?"

"Car accident, almost three years ago. A drunk driver jumped the light. They were killed instantly."

"I'm sorry." It's really all I can think of to say, as underwhelming as it may be.

"It's okay, it's in the past. I'm more concerned about the fact that I've missed twenty-four years of your life, that I can never get back."

"I know. Me too. But let's look on the bright side. Better late than never, right?"

. . .

TRYING to fit a lifetime's worth of information into one dinner is impossible, but we give it our best shot. Stephen tells me about Lucy and Hannah, the sister I can't seem to hear enough about. I learned that Sophie is married, with two teenaged boys. Not only have I just gained a sister, but two cousins, too. Bennett Communications is, as I'd suspected, a family business, and Stephen and Sophie had taken it over once their parents had died.

"We already had a fifty percent shareholding, and the balance we inherited when they died. Sophie still paints," he adds, "but only as a hobby, thank God. I'm running out of wall space. Sophie likes to gift us one of her paintings every Christmas. She did a portrait of Hannah last year that Hannah refused to let us hang. She said it made her look like a forty-year-old prostitute. Sophie wasn't amused. To be honest, she's never really been very good. Nowhere near your mother's league, at least."

I shrewdly changed the subject, veering it away from my mother. I told him about college, my business, my friends. We bond over the fact that we both like our toast slightly burnt at the edges, and discover we shared a passion for technology. I don't mention Blake. And worse, I don't tell him about Aaron. I don't tell my father that I had been married, or that I'm separated and filing for divorce. I don't want to face the questions that I know he'll ask, and ruin a perfect evening with the ugly truth of my failure.

IT'S past eleven when Stephen pays the bill. We're the last table to leave, and then only because the staff are waiting around at the bar, casting us dirty looks for keeping them so late.

"I feel like there's so much more to say," Stephen tells me as we walk to the door. I know exactly what he means. We hadn't stopped talking for hours, and I still craved so much more.

When we emerge onto the street, I catch sight of a dark blue pick-up parked at the curb. As I meet the eyes of the tall, dark-haired man leaning against it, my heart stutters in my chest.

"Blake?" I don't dare get my hopes up. Beside me, Stephen smiles.

"I'll see you next week, Catrina," he murmurs. We'd made arrangements to have dinner with his wife, Lucy, and my sister, Hannah, next Friday night.

Not taking my eyes off Blake, I reply. "I wouldn't miss it for the world."

Stephen gives Blake a nod, which Blake returns, and then saunters down the street to hunt for a cab. I put one foot in front of the other, trying to remember how to breathe, until I'm standing only a few feet away from Blake.

"How did it go?" he asks. His voice is strained, weary.

"It went really well. He was nice. Nothing like before."

"I suspected as much. He seemed completely different when we spoke on the phone."

I cast around for something else to say. "I have a sister."

His lips tug upward. "You have a sister?"

"Yes. Her name is Hannah. I'm meeting her next weekend."

"That's incredible. I'm really happy for you, Cat." Happy *for* me. Not happy *with* me. We gaze at each other in silent torment.

"What are you doing here?" I ask when I can't take it anymore.

"I needed to see you. To see if you were okay." He rubs his hand over the five o'clock shadow darkening his jaw. I'm too terrified to speak, for fear that he'll leave, but at the same time, I want to beg him to stay. He looks torn. Torn, and angry, and resigned. And I hate that I'm the reason for it.

"I need you to know how sorry I am," I begin cautiously. When he doesn't reply, I gather my courage and proceed. "I know what I did was awful. I know that what I've done is unforgivable. But I also know that I made a decision to be better, and that's exactly what I'm going to do. From the moment I made that decision, I ended things with Aaron. I need you to know that. Even if you don't believe anything else I say, please believe that."

"I do believe you," he seethes, and I can't tell if his anger is directed at me or himself. “I’ve been replaying that conversation we had at the hospital, over and over in my head, and do you know the one thing that keeps coming back to haunt me?”

“What?” I whisper.

“That you told me I didn’t deserve you. That you told me you didn’t want to get back together yet, that you weren’t ready. How you tried to keep me at arm’s length, even at that shitty B&B. And now I understand why.”

“I’m sorry.”

“Stop saying that!”

“So” I manage to stop myself just in time.

“I should have listened to you. I’m the one who instigated things in that bar. If I’d just listened to you, if I’d given you time...” he trails off, confusion etched in every inch of his face. “I don’t even know what to think anymore.”

“You didn’t do anything wrong.”

“I know that, too. But I also can’t deny that you tried to set things right. At the end. And that’s what makes this so God-damned difficult.”

Hope, bright and beautiful, burgeons in my chest.

“What are you saying?”

“I don’t know. I just know that I’ve never been so unhappy in my life. And it’s fucking cold out here.” He turns to the pick-up and opens the passenger door. “Get in.”

I don’t need to be told twice. I vault forward and leap inside. A moment later, Blake guns the engine.

We drive in silence for a long while. The smell of his cologne fills the small space and, with it, a pang of longing so fierce I feel dizzy.

“Was it the sex?” Blake says after a time. He winces as he says it. “I need straight answers, Cat,” he adds coldly when I don’t reply.

“Yes.”

He nods. “Are you still in love with him?”

“No. I don’t think I ever was. But...” I take a deep breath. This is the time for truth, as painful as it might be. “I don’t think he’s ever going to let me go. I don't want him, I swear it on my life, but he doesn't believe me."

We pull up to my apartment block, and I want to weep with relief when Blake steers us into the underground lot. He parks in his usual spot, but instead of getting out, he kills the engine and swivels to face me. I can't tell what he's thinking, as I swallow down the lump in my throat.

"I only have two questions," Blake says. "Yes or no, that's all I want to hear from you. Got it?"

I nod my head.

"Is it over?"

"Yes." There's not a trace of doubt in my voice.

"Do you love me?"

"More than you could possibly know." I can't help the raw emotion that surges up and stings my eyes. Blake watches as the tears well, and then gives me a tentative smile.

"That wasn't a yes or a no."

"Yes."

He presses his lips together. Stares at me. Seems to come to a decision, and then opens his door. I hold my breath as he rounds the car and opens mine. When he offers me his hand, a dozen butterflies take flight in my stomach. And as we walk, hand in hand, to the elevator, the world seems to re-align.

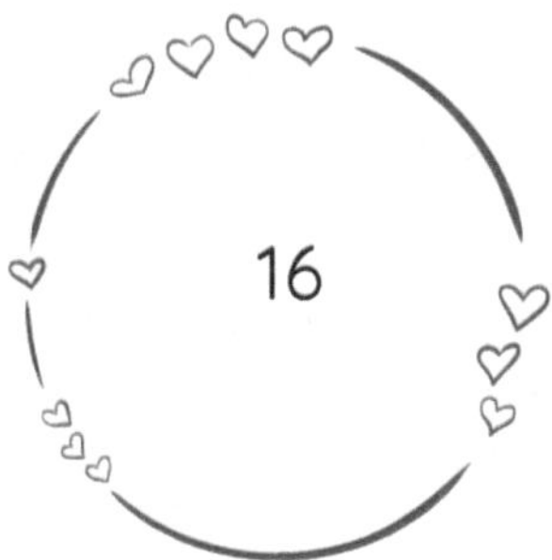

"That is the most romantic thing I've ever heard," Gwen sighs, as I relay the story to her and Bianca. We're at 1954, an upmarket, All-American bistro with a fifties flair. I've spent the past hour telling them about mine and Blake's reunion. Of course, I've omitted the part about Aaron. I just told them Blake and I had broken up after a huge fight, but I'd gone into great detail about how we got back together.

"It was," I sigh. It's impossible to put into words how relieved I am that Blake understood that I had chosen him.

"I still can't believe you found your dad," Bianca quips.

"He's flying in on Friday," I say. It's been a week since my dinner with Stephen. A week since Blake brought me home and stayed. Seven long nights, each better than the one before.

"Wipe that look off your face," Bianca says, grinning. "You're making me uncomfortable."

"I can't help it."

"Try. I have news, too, and I'm going to need you to pay attention."

Automatically, Gwen and I both look at her left hand, but her ring finger is bare.

"God no," Bianca whines. "Not that. What is wrong with you two?"

"You can't blame us for hoping," Gwen says.

"How many times do I need to tell you, I don't believe in marriage."

"What's the news, then?" Gwen asks, but I'm focused on Bianca, my brain going a mile a minute. It takes me a second to notice her untouched wine glass, and another to register what it means, but she's already blurted it out.

"I'm pregnant."

The squeal of excitement that follows draws the attention of every diner in the restaurant, but I don't care. I'm already on my feet, Gwen a second behind me, and we're hugging Bianca, who remains seated.

"I kind of wish I'd kept my fat mouth shut," she grumbles.

"This is the best news!" Gwen laughs. "Mike must be over the moon."

"He's got morning sickness," Bianca says. "And he's been strutting around like the cock amidst the chickens since we found out. You'd swear I had nothing to do with it, the way he's behaving."

"Stop it," I chide, still laughing. Mike dotes on Bianca, a miracle, given how she treats him. I glance down at her flat stomach. "I can't actually believe it. How far along are you?"

"Only eight weeks. We just found out. And I've already gained five pounds." She gives a groan off despair. "I'm going to be fat, you guys. I'm going to be one of those women who blows up like a bullfrog and spends the rest of her life battling the bulge."

"You're not going to get fat!" Gwen insists.

"And even if you do," I add, "it'll be worth it. You're having a baby, Biancs! A baby!"

Bianca throws me a filthy look. "I really should have kept my damn mouth shut."

"You're going to have to marry Mike now," I tease, knowing it'll infuriate her even more.

"Catrina, I swear if you don't stop I'm going to punch you in the face."

I feign outraged indignance. "You're with child, Bianca. Remember, the baby will pick up on your emotions, so you should be channeling positivity and light. You should also sing to it, lullabies, preferably, and as often as you can."

Gwen is laughing too hard to comment.

THE REST of the evening is dominated by baby talk, much to Bianca's disgust, but it's inevitable that the subject of Aaron will rear its ugly head. It's Bianca who brings him up, no doubt her way of getting back at me for harping on about all things pre and postnatal.

"He asked after you the other day," she tells me, taking a tiny but defiant sip of her wine. "My gynae said it's fine in moderation," she snaps, as Gwen's eyes widen. "Anyway, Mike was a bit shocked because Aaron doesn't usually mention you, but he wanted to know if you were still seeing Blake."

It's a good feeling, to have Aaron brought up in conversation and not feel a crippling desire to know everything he might have said about me. To be frank, I'd rather be talking about babies.

"I don't really care what Aaron says or does," I reply. "Not anymore. I filed for divorce."

"You *what*?" They chorus.

I shrug. "It's long overdue. Aaron and I aren't getting back together, and I'm tired of living in limbo."

"Wow," Gwen breathes. "I mean, I know you're right, but it just seems so final."

"It was final the day I caught him with Staci. It just took me a while to figure that out."

"I'm not judging you, Cat. I'm proud of you." She steels herself and then declares, "Aaron's an asshole." It's so out of character that Bianca and I are shocked into temporary silence.

Bianca finds her tongue first. "Gwendolyn Jones!" she squawks. "You better not let Jason hear you talking about his bestie like that."

Gwen grins. "It's true, though. He was a bastard to Cat. And if I'm being honest, I can't stand Jason spending time with him. I don't doubt for a second that he's unfaithful to Staci, too, and every time he takes Jason out for a drink I get a sick feeling in my stomach."

"Jason would never cheat on you," I say honestly, even as a kernel of guilt forms in my stomach. Aaron does cheat on Staci – I know, because I've experienced it first-hand.

"I know he wouldn't," Gwen says, "but that doesn't mean I want him hanging around other women through Aaron."

"You should come to dinner with me and Blake. Both of you, with Mike and Jason. They'll like him," I promise. "And maybe, just maybe, we can start our own circle. Blake would never behave like Aaron, he's a good guy. Unless you guys don't want to..." I add, uncertainly, when neither of them respond.

"We totally want to," Bianca clarifies. "We just thought you'd never ask."

"Why do you think we keep coming to dinner?" Bianca says, "and keeping this friendship alive? We've been waiting for you to offer for months."

"I was starting to wonder if Blake really existed, or if he was just someone you made up to make yourself look good," Gwen teases.

"What are you guys talking about? You've met him!"

"Once," she counters. "And for all we know he could've been one of your clients."

I frown. Surely it's been more than that. We had lunch a few months ago, but now that I think about it, I can't recall a single time since then that Blake and my friends were in the same room together. "Really? We've been together over six months."

Bianca gives me a pointed look. "Exactly."

"Right, then, dinner it is. We're starting a new circle. Would the guys go for that?"

"Jason doesn't have a choice," Gwen says. "God knows I have to put up with Staci more often than I care to count."

"Mike will be there," Bianca grins, rubbing at her belly. "Where the baby goes, Mike follows."

With all the pieces of my life falling so seamlessly into place, the only dark cloud hanging over my head is the fact that I still haven't spoken to my mother. Blake insists that I should leave it alone, and let her come to me, but the longer we go without speaking, the more I worry about her. Her self-destructive behavior is always worse when she's in an anxious state, and I feel terrible for disclosing that I'm the one who's been buying her paintings. My mother, for all her faults, suffers from crippling self-doubt. I wouldn't be surprised if she never picks up a paintbrush again after this.

My grandparents have seen her, and Grams assures me that she seems fine, but it's hard to believe, considering the source. Grams is a little naïve to my mother's indulgent behavior, and operates on a strict ignorance is bliss policy.

"At least wait until Monday," Blake tells me on Friday night. We're on our way to meet Stephen and his family for dinner, and I'm cradling my phone in my lap, willing it to ring. I've pulled my mother's name up so many times today, but I haven't summoned the courage to hit the call button. "Give her another few days. I know this is eating you up inside, but calling her now and brushing everything that's happened under the rug isn't going to do either of you any favors in the long run."

"I'm worried about her."

He reaches out and gives my knee a squeeze. "I know. But no news is good news, right?"

"True." I shove my phone back into my purse and straighten my shoulders. "It's been this long, what harm could a few more days do?"

We pull up outside the hotel, and a valet steps forward to take care of our parking.

"I can't believe I'm meeting my sister," I tell Blake, as we step into an expensive foyer which smells of orange blossom and money. "What do you think she'll be like?"

"If she's anything like you, she'll be adorable," he says.

IT TURNS out adorable is not a word I'd use to describe Hannah Bennett. We're not even halfway to the table when a streak of red barrels toward me, and a miniature version of myself throws her arms around my neck.

"Catrina!" she shrieks, letting me go for only a second to get a good look at my face, before pinning me in another bear hug. "Oh my God, you look just like me! This is too much, isn't this too much? I can't actually believe it, I swear when dad told me I almost had a shit-fit!" she continues on, but she's speaking so quickly I barely catch a word of it.

"Hannah, language!" a stern voice chides. I look up, to find a slim, attractive woman at Hannah's shoulder. She offers me a smile that doesn't quite meet her eyes. "You must be Catrina," she says, in a practiced voice. "I'm Lucy, Stephen's wife." She holds out her hand, and I disentangle one of my arms to shake it.

"It's really good to meet you, Lucy," I say. Her hand trembles slightly in mine, which I take as a good sign. It means she might be nervous, as opposed to unfriendly.

Hannah releases her vice grip from my neck, but slips her arm through mine and insists on walking beside me. Stephen, on his feet at the table, smiles at the sight.

"You two look even more alike than I thought," he says. He drops a quick kiss on my forehead when I hug him hello, the action as natural as breathing, and then turns to shake Blake's hand. "Nice to see you again, Blake."

"You too, Mr. Bennett."

"Stephen, please. This is my wife, Lucy, and this little firecracker," he adds, ruffling Hannah's hair, "is Hannah."

Hannah ducks away and swats at her middle parting. "Jeez, Dad! Do you mind? I'm sixteen, not six! No, you're not there," she adds, as I start to sit. "You're here, next to me."

"Sweetheart, Catrina can decide where she wants to sit," Lucy says. Hannah gives her an insolent glare.

"Yes, and she wants to sit next to me. Right, Cat?"

I try to stifle my laughter, but Hannah's wicked grin tells me she sees right through me.

"Next to you is perfect," I say. Even Lucy smiles.

IT'S A MAGICAL EVENING. Perhaps it's the sense of family that I've lacked for so long, or just the fact the Bennetts are genuinely nice people, who have embraced me as one of their own, but by the time our main courses arrive, my emotional cup is full. I feel sublimely happy. Until Aaron walks through the door, Staci barnacled to his side.

Blake doesn't notice, or at least, I don't think he does. Aaron's table is behind him and slightly to the left, so unless he turns around the chances are good that he won't. From my seat, however, I have a clear view of them. My euphoria vanishes.

Staci has her back to me. Aaron, on the other hand, looks directly at me as he sits down. For just a second, his face registers shock, and then my stomach clenches as his lips curve upward in a predatory smile. This is exactly the type of situation Aaron gets off on. I did too, not so long ago, but the thought of what's going on inside his head right now makes me sick. Deliberately, I turn my attention back to the others, but I can still feel his eyes boring into me.

I wait until everyone has finished their main course before I make my move.

"Can we trade seats for a bit?" I ask Hannah. "I'd like to talk to Stephen, if that's okay?"

She doesn't bat an eyelid, although Lucy looks slightly alarmed.

"Sure!" Hannah says, getting to her feet so fast she almost upends the table. Then she pauses, a small frown creasing her smooth brow. "Why do you call him that?"

"Who?"

"Dad. You call him Stephen."

The table falls silent, and I feel my cheeks grow hot. I'm sure Stephen doesn't expect me to call him Dad, certainly not so soon, and I'm definitely not comfortable with it either.

"Um..." I trail off, casting a helpless look at Blake, but he seems at a loss for words too. Stephen suddenly develops an intense interest in his own fingernails.

"Hannah, honey," Lucy intervenes gently, "this is all very new, for all of us. Catrina might not be comfortable calling your father Dad just yet."

Or ever, I think to myself, in a panic. It's not that I don't like him, because the opposite is true, but it would feel forced.

Hannah pulls a face, one that I've noticed she uses mostly on her mother. "Whatever. It's weird."

She takes my recently vacated seat and immediately starts bending Blake's ear about surgery, and whether it's anything like you see on *Grey's Anatomy*. Hearing her mention the on-call rooms, I see Blake's ears pink. *Yes*, I could tell her, based on my own experience, *that really does happen*. But I don't, obviously.

"Sorry about that," Stephen says, once he's sure Hannah is fully invested in her conversation and not eavesdropping on ours. "She can be a bit blunt."

"Situation normal for a sixteen-year-old. Trust me, I know. I was impossible at her age."

"Tell me more about your childhood," he says, refilling my glass.

"What do you want to know?" This topic could navigate us into treacherous waters. I answer him as best I can without mentioning my mother, but my answers are superficial at best, and I can tell he's not satisfied.

"I'm just going to use the ladies," I say brightly, needing a reprieve. Stephen and Blake both get to their feet as I do, and I smile at the chivalrous gesture. Hannah makes to follow me, but her mother places a firm hand on her arm.

"Let her at least go to the bathroom in peace," she says firmly.

"I'll be right back," I tell Hannah, and then shoot Lucy a grateful smile.

The bathroom is all white – white tiled floors, white wallpaper with a thin silver foil, and white handtowels, which are disposed of in a white wicker basket beside the sink. I splash some water on my face and dab it dry, careful not to ruin my make-up, and then head back outside. I've only stepped out into the hall when a hand seizes my shoulder and pushes me back up against the wall. It doesn't hurt, but it's rough enough to mean business.

"Aaron!" I gasp, startled out of my wits. "What the hell do you think you're doing?"

"What do you think?" he grins, utterly confident. With his free hand, he pushes open the bathroom door to check if there's anyone inside. I have no doubt that the second he's certain of it, he'll try to maneuver me inside.

I don't give him the opportunity. Wedging both hands between us, I shove at his chest. "Get off me!" Thankfully, the force drives him backward, giving me just enough room to slip past him. I haven't taken two steps when he seizes my wrist.

"Where do you think you're going?" he asks. He strokes the

length of my side with his free hand, from ribs to waist in a playful gesture filled with promise.

"Let me go," I growl, trying to shake him off.

This time, he's genuinely bewildered. Aaron would never hurt me, but he's so used to getting his own way that it would never occur to him that I don't want this. We've played this game for so long my denial may as well be foreplay.

"Get your hands off my daughter." It's a low growl, from not three feet away. We whirl to find Stephen blocking the hall, a menacing look on his face. Aaron drops my hand like a hornet's nest. His head whips from me to Stephen and then back again, in search of answers.

"Your daughter?" he asks, eventually.

"Yes," Stephen says, holding his ground. "My daughter." He offers me his hand, and I snatch hold of it, letting him draw me to the safety of his side. "And who the hell are you?"

Aaron regains a bit of his swagger. "I'm her husband."

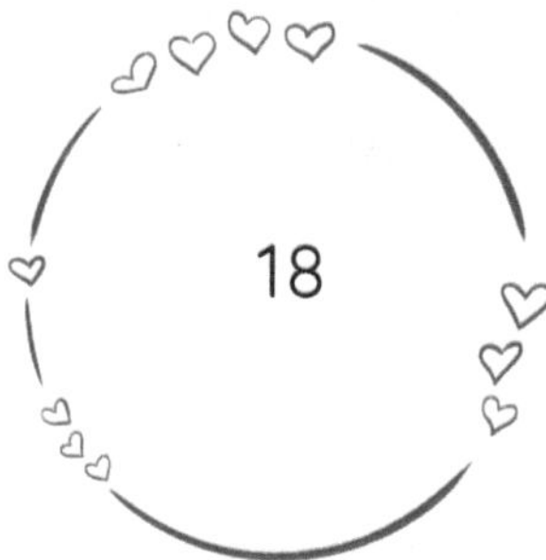

18

Blake is furious. Furious that Aaron was at the restaurant in the first place, furious that he would dare pull such a dirty trick, and mostly, furious that he wasn't there to protect me. Sensing that something was amiss when Stephen and I returned, Lucy had wisely hauled Hannah off to bed right after dessert. Hannah didn't go willingly. Aaron had done the same with Staci, only they'd skipped eating altogether, and Staci didn't put up much of a fight. I don't know what he told her, or if she even knew I was there, not that it matters. By the time Lucy and Hannah had gone, and I'd filled Blake in on what had happened, Aaron had vanished, along with Blake's opportunity to confront him.

"We can't carry on like this," he seethes. His hands are clenched into fists on the table, and I slip my own into them, slowly easing the tension out.

"You're going to need to explain this to me, Cat," Stephen says. His words are gentle, but firm, brooking no room for argument.

I take a deep breath. "Aaron *is* my husband, technically, but I've filed for divorce. We've been separated for over a year." I don't elaborate. There's no way I'm explaining that I was still sleeping with

Aaron up until a few weeks ago. "Aaron had an affair," I say instead, not feeling the least bit guilty that I'm throwing him under the bus. "That's how it ended."

"It didn't look like it had ended," Stephen points out. "At least not from his perspective."

"He's not happy about the divorce. But that doesn't mean he wants us to get back together," I add hastily. "Aaron doesn't want me. He just can't handle the thought of me being with someone else."

"Is he dangerous?" Stephen asks. "I mean, exactly how worried should I be?" The strain in his voice makes me smile. He's acting like a protective dad, and even though this is by far one of the most uncomfortable conversations of my life, it feels nice to be worried about.

"You have nothing to worry about. He's not dangerous, he's just a dick."

"I can handle Aaron," Blake says darkly.

"I'd be more than happy to help," Stephen adds, and they share a look.

"I'm just sorry our evening was ruined," I say sadly. I'm more angry about that than what Aaron did. "I was really enjoying myself."

Stephen manages a small smile. "There'll be plenty more like this. In fact, I've been thinking about a few things. Blake, you mentioned you'll be applying at a number of hospitals? Have you given any thought to California?"

I go rigid in my seat. Stephen must notice because he hastens to explain. "I'm sorry, I'm not telling either of you what to do. I just thought... well, Long Beach is really beautiful in the summer, and to be frank, Cat, I'd love to have you close by. I want to get to know you – to really get to know you, and it'd be a whole lot easier if you weren't four hundred miles away. It's your decision, obviously, but I want you to consider all your options, and know that you have options on the West Coast. You have a family, who would love to have you around." He smiles at me, and it's a smile that tells me how badly he wants this, how desperately he wants me in his life, not only for the occasional weekend, and special occasions, but as a permanent fixture.

So, rather than deny him outright, I find myself saying, "how would Lucy feel about that?"

"DID YOU MEAN WHAT YOU SAID?" Blake asks me on the drive home. "Would you really consider moving to California?"

"I didn't think I would," I admit, "but I'd already decided I'd follow you anywhere, and if anywhere happened to be closer to Stephen, it'd be even better. I don't know," I add, as he gives me a wry look, "I just want to know them. I want to be there, for Hannah especially. I want to be the big sister who offers advice about boys, and who lets her borrow my clothes. I know it sounds corny, but"

"It doesn't sound corny at all," he interrupts. "Family is everything, Cat. You're allowed to want what everyone else takes for granted."

"What about your parents, then?' I challenge. "Shouldn't you be looking for a job in Sacramento?"

"I grew up with my parents," he reminds me, "I haven't missed anything. And it just so happens that two of my hospitals of choice are in California."

"Well in that case," I say, with a surge of delight, "you should definitely apply."

He doesn't bring up Aaron until we're home. I knew he wouldn't let it go for long, but I'm glad he waited until we were curled up on the couch in our pajamas, because I have a plan of my own to get rid of Aaron once and for all, and I know he's not going to like it.

His response is as predictable as it is vehement. "No way. There's no way I'm letting you do that. I'll talk to him. Trust me, when I'm done he'll leave you alone."

I don't doubt that Blake could intimidate Aaron, but the problem is, that I don't. I'm the one who Aaron feels he can push around, and until he learns otherwise, this will never be over.

"You can't be with me twenty-four-seven," I say. "He'll find a way to get me on my own. That's what he does. *I* need to do this. I need to take back my life, not have my boyfriend do it for me."

"You shouldn't have to do anything. You've told him it's over. It should be enough."

"It's more complicated than that." I cringe, because what I mean is that I've told Aaron numerous times that it's over, only to go crawling back to him. It's not surprising that he doesn't believe me now - I'm like the little boy who cried wolf. Blake's scowl assures me that he knows exactly what I mean, but he holds his tongue.

"I *want* to do this, Blake. I'm *going* to do it. For me, not for you," I add meaningfully. "I'm not asking for your permission, but I would like your approval."

He exhales a resigned breath. "So long as we're clear, I don't like it."

I poke him between the ribs. "Oh come on. You like it a little bit."

He gives me an arch look. "I really don't."

"It's nothing less than he deserves," I say. "It's high time Aaron had a taste of his own medicine."

I HAVE to wait a week to put my plan into action. Now that I've made the decision, I want to get it over with as soon as possible, especially after the two text messages that I get from Aaron over the weekend, which I don't tell Blake about. I meant what I said to Blake, about taking my life back, but he has no idea just how deep my resolve lies. He could never fully understand how much Aaron has taken from me over the years – how he chipped away at my self-confidence, at my sense of self-worth. How he played on my vulnerability and my desperate need to feel loved. Aaron didn't give a damn about how my mother treated me, it only made me that much more malleable, like putty in his hands. And his affection was my reward for good behavior, the sick bastard. Aaron twisted me into something ugly, but now that Blake has shown me that I'm worthy of being loved, I'm learning to love myself again. I am no longer Aaron's plaything. He's taken too much, and, in just a few days, I get to take it all back. To be free of him once and for all.

ON MONDAY MORNING, just as I'm bracing myself for the dreaded phone call to my mother, I get a call from Trish at the gallery.

"Catrina, you're an extremely valued client," she begins, after the pleasantries are over. "I thought long and hard about making this call, but I realized I have no choice."

"What is it?" I ask with a sigh. "Did another Viola Davis painting come in?"

"Actually, more than one," Trish says, but before I can express my surprise, she's talking again. "I am so very sorry to have to tell you this, but Viola has issued strict instruction that you are not permitted to buy any more of her work. I don't know how she found out," she adds quickly, defending her gallery, and her reputation, "I can promise you I would never disclose an anonymous buyer's information."

"It's okay," I say, letting her off the hook. "I know you didn't tell her."

"I can't think why she would want to exclude such a fan of her work," Trish tuts. I'm pretty sure her disappointment has more to do with the commission she's going to lose, than my lack of access to Viola's paintings, but it's sincere, nonetheless. "Such a pity, too," Trish sighs, "as the showcase opened today. I just wanted to let you know before you read about it in the papers."

"What are you talking about? What showcase?"

"The Viola Davis exhibition. I assumed you'd have heard, given what a huge fan you are of her work."

"You're exhibiting her work? Like, a full exhibition, not just a single painting?"

"Yes. She brought them in a few weeks ago and we signed her up immediately. Even I have to admit, they're incredible. So different from her usual work, but utterly captivating. Perhaps if I spoke to her again"

But I don't wait to hear what Trish proposes, and I end the call without another word. I'm already walking out of my apartment, snatching up my purse as I go. I catch a cab and bite agonizingly at my nails as we get stuck behind one slow-moving vehicle after another. I tap my foot impatiently, cursing my bad luck. Eventually, when we're only a few blocks away, I tell the cabbie to stop, and I hand over the fare. It'll be quicker to walk the rest of the way.

A GORGEOUS SIGNBOARD sits outside the gallery entrance, heralding the exhibition of incredible local talent, Viola Davis. Seeing my mother's name in print, validated by such a respected establishment, brings tears of pride to my eyes. I slip inside behind a tall, bespectacled man carrying a camera bag. A press pass hangs from the lanyard around his neck. Trish is busy with a customer, and another is waiting in line. I keep my head down and turn my back to her, while surreptitiously scanning the walls.

"Holy shit," I breathe, forgetting that I'm supposed to be hiding from Trish. I turn a full 360 degrees, my eyes feasting on the riot of color which adorns the walls. A bunch of lilies in full bloom, in a cracked bottle-green vase. A pink buckled bicycle, with streamers made of old newspaper, rippling in the wind. A rusted swing set, with an apricot silk scarf where the chain should be. An overgrown lawn, rampant with sunflowers. A silver station wagon, the fender dented. And in every single one, a redheaded child. I'm watering the lilies with an ancient, rusted watering can. Riding the bicycle, in a white broderie anglaise dress, red braids flying behind me, parallel to the makeshift streamers. I'm on the swing, feet pointed toward the sky, reaching higher than ever. I know that not five minutes later, the apricot scarf will rip, and I will crash to the ground in a heap, my wrist broken. I'm walking between the sunflowers, my eyes alight with wonder as I peer up at them, my hand brushing the green stalks. In the station wagon, I'm kissing a boy. He has blond hair and glasses, and I recognize him even though his face is in shadow. Neil O'Donnell, my first kiss.

My mother has painted my entire childhood, in frenzied, vibrant strokes. My life in color, a poignant reminder of details I'd long forgotten. I turn again, taking in every painting. I grow older, holding the hand of a man with a brittle smile and cold eyes. I marry him. The dress is beautiful, my face is not. Instead, I wear a halo of tears, and an expression of pain. I'm in a hospital bed, pale against the stark white sheets, but beautiful now. I'm smiling up at a man with a stethoscope around his neck. I turn on the spot, rotating slowly as I take in every exquisite detail, every truth my mother has laid bare on canvas, and my legs start to tremble beneath me.

"Catrina?" Trish's voice seems to be coming from far away. My head begins to pound, dark spots flickering in my peripheral vision. The girl in the paintings is smiling. Then she's not. My knees hit the hardwood floor. "Catrina!" Trish is at my side, frantic. My shoulders heave, wracking sobs consuming everything. "Call an ambulance!" Trish yells.

"No," I croak, shaking my head. Tears flow freely down my cheeks, blurring the sight of those beautiful, beautiful paintings. *She remembers.*

"Catrina, I need you to talk to me," Trish insists, her hands on my face, pulling it toward her. Through my tears, I smile, and then, as the beast which has been sitting on my chest, crushing me for years, unfurls itself, my tears give way to laughter.

"Cat!" Blake bellows, when he sees me being wheeled into the E.R on a stretcher. "What the hell happened?" I'm laughing, and crying, and far too hysterical to answer, so the kind-faced paramedic named Paul, who'd held my hand in the ambulance while I poured my heart out, does it for me.

"She's fine, she's just had a bit of an emotional breakdown."

Blake is at my side, his face assessing mine. "Let's get her into a bed." He leads the way to a private room, then lifts me off the stretcher and onto the bed. "Thanks for your help," he tells the paramedics.

"Just doing our job," Paul replies. His associate leaves without a word, but before he goes, Paul gives me a brief pat on the leg. "You look after yourself, Miss."

"I'll be right back," Blake tells me. He steps into the hall to speak to the nurse on duty in a low voice. I hear her raised protests, but Blake cuts her off. "I need ten minutes." He's back almost immediately, closing the door behind him. He stands over me, his eyes filled with concern. "What happened?" he murmurs softly. "Is it Aaron? Did something happen?"

I shake my head, no.

"Your mom?"

I nod, and promptly burst into fresh tears, which galvanize Blake into action. He opens a cabinet on the far side of the room and roots around for a minute before withdrawing a syringe and a small vial.

"I'm going to give you something, okay? To calm you down."

I manage another bob of my head.

"I'm sorry Cat, but I need your verbal consent."

"Yes." My voice is hoarse, and barely audible, but it's all he needs. He rolls me gently onto my side and I feel the prick of the needle in my backside.

The effect is instantaneous. A warm, fuzziness spreads from the source of the jab to envelop my whole body, and I slump back on the bed. I feel as though I've just woken up, or am just about to fall asleep. It's a heady calm.

"Wow. That's lovely."

"It packs quite a punch," Blake agrees. He disposes of the needle and comes to sit beside me on the bed. I scoot over to make room, but my movements feel sluggish and uncoordinated.

"Tell me what happened," he says. And this time, I do. It takes some time, and I shed a few more tears, but I get it out eventually.

"What do you think it means?" he asks gently when I'm done. I think he already knows the answer, but he wants me to say it.

"I think, in her own way, my mother loves me."

His smile is dazzling. "I think she does, too," he says, pulling me against his chest. I bury my face in his scrubs. "Do you remember that night I drove her home?"

"Mmmm," I murmur.

"I lied to you. I told you that nothing she said would make you feel better, but that wasn't true. I just didn't want to tell you because I thought it would be best if you heard it from her."

I lift my face to meet his gaze. "What did she say?"

"A lot. But in a nutshell, that the real reason she didn't want you to meet your father, was because she was terrified of losing you."

I think about how quickly I'd been ready to pack up and move to Long Beach. "She wasn't wrong. After everything she's done, Stephen seemed like a knight in shining armor."

"He's your father, Cat. He cares about you. It's not an act. And I do still think it would be good for you to get out of this place. To leave all the bullshit behind and start afresh."

"But?"

His chest rises and falls beneath my hand. "But I think it would destroy you to abandon Viola. No matter what she's done."

"You're saying I should stay?"

"I'm saying we should figure out what's best for both of us before we make any decisions."

He's right, as usual.

THE VIOLA DAVIS exhibition sold out in under a week. Trish, having finally discovered my true identity, texted me to let me know that the gallery was planning another in the fall. I still haven't spoken to my mother, but Grams let me know that she'd asked to move back home, just for a couple of months, to "get her stuff together" as Grams so eloquently put it. I'd decided to give her space. If she wanted to talk to me, she would. Even after the revelation of seeing her paintings, I didn't reach out. I was working through my demons, and she needed to work through hers. I could only hope that she'd be ready to talk when she had. I suspected she would. It's what I would do, and I was, after all, my mother's child. For now, I was just taking things one day at a time. And today, it just so happens that I face my final hurdle. The final barrier between me and my new life. I'd waited longer than a week, but as I had so recently learned, late was always better than never.

I CLIMB the steps to Aaron's apartment with a clear head and a clear conscience. He started texting me again after the night he'd seen me with my father. I'd read every single one, letting his words fuel the flame of my determination. He'd also fired back a legal letter to my attorneys. He was contesting the divorce. That had been the final nail in his coffin.

I lift my hand to the door to knock. Two short taps, followed by a pause. Another single tap. Our secret code. Aaron's face blazes triumphant as he jerks open the door.

"Kitty Cat," he croons. "What took you so long?"

I don't make it easy for him. He'd see through that. I stride inside and fix him with the most furious look I can muster.

"This has gone on long enough, Aaron," I snap, dumping my purse on the dining table. "You need to sign the papers. I'm not going to ask you again."

"How's your doctor friend?" he asks, blatantly ignoring me. "I do hope I didn't cause too much trouble when last we met."

I cock my head and regard him levelly.

"Actually, you didn't. Blake moved in last weekend."

The spark flares in his eyes. Anger, because Blake has moved in on his territory. Lust, because Blake still wants me.

"You really shouldn't lead him on like that, Cat." His eyes are roaming the length of my body. My outfit, so carefully selected, for the tightness of the blouse and the short length of the skirt, is taking effect.

"Just sign the God-damned papers, Aaron."

"Fine," he says. I stand rooted to the spot. This wasn't what I'd anticipated. "If," Aaron croons, and I exhale in relief, "you give me one last kiss."

"I'm not playing this game."

"Aw, come on. What harm could it do? If you're so obviously over me, and you really want this divorce, what difference would one little kiss make? We could call it a goodbye."

"Fine," I snap. "If that's what it takes, what the hell. But you swear you'll sign the papers?"

He holds up his hand. "Scout's honor."

"You could never be a boy scout, Aaron." I take a steadying breath and walk toward him. He stays where he is, lounging against the back of the couch, his hands in his pockets. Bastard. When I'm only inches away, I lean forward and kiss him chastely on the cheek.

"There. Happy now?"

"Not a chance, sweetheart." He's really enjoying himself now. "I know your boyfriend's probably as vanilla as they come, but surely you haven't forgotten everything I taught you."

"Aaron"

"A deal's a deal, Cat. Unless deep down, you don't really want me to sign those papers?"

Furiously, I reach up and seize him around the neck, before sliding my fingers up into his hair. I yank a fistful, hard enough that it brings tears to his eyes, and Aaron hisses.

"That's better," he sneers. "Perhaps you haven't forgot"

I don't let him finish. I'm already pressing my lips to his, parting them instantly as his tongue darts out to sweep my mouth. Aaron groans, low and deep in his throat, and then his arms come around me. I can feel his need, straining against his zipper. Without warning, he shoves his hands beneath the waistband of my skirt and slides them over my backside, lower and lower, until his fingers brush my core. I leap back, shoving at his chest so hard he almost falls backward over the couch.

"What the hell, Cat?" he thunders.

I give him a pained look, my chest heaving. "Stay away from me," I croak.

Comprehension dawns on his face and his own lips curve upward. "Why? Are you struggling to keep your hands to yourself, sweetheart? Where's all that fiery determination now?"

"Just sign the papers, Aaron." But it's useless. He knows he's got me exactly where he wants me, and he stalks toward me like a predator advancing on its prey.

I try one last time. "Please let me go."

"Not a chance. You belong to *me*." His eyes are liquid with desire, and my pulse is racing frantically as I try to find an escape route.

"There's nowhere to run," Aaron taunts, drawing so close that I can smell his cologne. "And even if there was, what are you running from? You'll never find this with anyone else. Let me love you, Cat. You know how good it'll be." At that, he reaches for me, his big hands lifting me clear off my feet before he traps me against his chest. "What are you going to do now?" he asks, his eyes probing mine. Beneath the challenge glimmering in the blue depths, there's tenderness too. In his own twisted way, Aaron does love me, but it's not the love I need. Not anymore.

"I don't know," I whisper. "What am I going to do now, Aaron?" My chest is still heaving, rubbing against his own with every inhalation. His mouth crashes down onto mine, and I resist for only a second before I melt against him. I arch my body against his, our tongues engaged in frantic swordplay. I fumble for his shirt and pull it over his head. The brief moment our lips are parted is too long, and he claims my mouth again immediately, even as he kicks off his pants.

My groan is his undoing. He yanks at my clothing, his hands warm against my bare skin.

"Slowly," I breathe into his mouth. His answering groan is pained. I kiss his neck, then trace circles with my tongue, moving lazily lower, down his neck, over the hollow of his throat. His hands are everywhere, touching every inch of me he can reach, but I twist away, playing coy, making him work for it. He's becoming frantic, his fingers biting into my soft skin, and I'm starting to worry that it will all be over too quickly, when finally, mercifully, I hear the door open behind me.

Aaron's expression, as he catches sight of Staci, is priceless. It's Friday, after all. She shouldn't be back for hours. But it had taken just one call from me, half an hour ago, for her to hurry home.

I don't wait for Staci's wrath. With a small smile up at Aaron, I scoop up my clothes, wrap my coat around myself, and retrieve my purse from the table.

"Aaron refuses to give me a divorce," I tell Staci as I pass her on my way to the door. I pluck the letter from his attorney from my purse and hand it to her. She doesn't look at it. She only has eyes for Aaron, naked and guilty, standing immobile with shock.

"I was so sure you were lying." Her voice is small, and filled with pain.

"I'm sorry," I say. And I am. Not that she had to find out, but because I know she loves him.

"You bitch!" Aaron yells, regaining his voice only slightly too late, as I step out into the hall.

I EMERGE ONTO THE STREET, the weight of Aaron's hold over me gone. He will never hurt me again, never make me feel inferior, or that I'm not worthy of being loved for anything beyond my body and the things that I can do with it. He knows now, the lengths I will go to if he tries to force my hand again. As if on cue, Blake pushes off the pick-up and comes toward me, his eyes scanning me for any sign of ill-treatment.

"How did it go?" he asks. I know how badly it hurts him to know that Aaron has touched me, so I keep my distance, planting my heels a few feet away. It'll take a bit of time for him to be okay, but I'm not going anywhere. We have all the time in the world. Blake didn't want me to do this - hated that I was doing it, but ultimately, he understood that it wasn't just about Aaron getting caught. It was about humiliating him the way he had me for so long, and reclaiming my sense of self.

"He won't be bothering us anymore," I say.

Blake releases a slow breath and then a smile, honest and beautiful, creases his face. He takes in the crumpled ball of clothing in my hands, and his gaze lowers to the buttons of my coat. The knot in my stomach unravels under the intensity of that gaze as he reaches out his hands and loops them through the belt of my coat, pulling me toward him. So much for my theory that he'd take some time to get over it, I think wildly, as he pulls me in for a long, lingering kiss.

"Let's go home," he says when we break apart. His voice is hoarse. A sign just ahead catches my eye, and I lean over and toss my clothes into the front seat of the car. We're both acutely aware that I'm wearing nothing beneath the cream cashmere.

"I've got a better idea," I say, taking his hand. "Let's go get a drink."

THE END

ABOUT THE AUTHOR

Rachel Rhodes is a pseudonym for award-winning author, copywriter, and lover of the written word, Melissa Delport. She is published in both S.A and the U.S.A and offers professional copywriting services and author coaching.

For ten years she owned and operated her own specialized logistics company until she woke up one morning and decided it was time to put her English degree to good use.

Melissa lives with her husband and three teenagers, none of whom take her seriously.

She also writes romantic suspense as Lissa Del and contemporary romance as Rachel Rhodes.

For more information, visit www.melissadelport.com

ALSO BY RACHEL RHODES

ROMANCE & ROMANTIC COMEDY (as Rachel Rhodes)

Awkward in Print

Awkward Abroad

Awkward Infidelity

Awkward in Trouble

CONTEMPORARY WOMENS FICTION (as Lissa Del)

Rainfall

Riven

A Life Made of Lava

URBAN FANTASY

GUARDIANS OF SUMMERFELD SERIES

The Cathedral of Cliffdale (Book 1)

The Fight of the Fallen (Book 2)

The Hope of Hawkstone (Book 3)

The Balance of the Blood (Book 4)

Full Series Boxed Set (Books 1-4)

SHADOW MAGIC SERIES

The Witchborn Curse (Book 1)

The Shadow Huntress (Book 2)

The Charmed Quarter (Book 3)

The Rogue Coven (Book 4)

The Darkest Realm (Book 5)

The Hybrid's Fate (Book 6)

Full Series Boxed Set (Books 1-6)

THE TRAVELER DUOLOGY

The Traveler (Book 1)

The Survivor (Book 1.5)

The Saviour (Book 2)

TIME TRAVEL FANTASY

The Clock Keeper

DYSTOPIAN

THE LEGACY TRILOGY

The Legacy (Legacy Trilogy Book 1)

The Legion (Legacy Trilogy Book 2)

The Legend (Legacy Trilogy Book 3)

ANTHOLOGIES

The Space Between Dreams & Chaos

The Space Between Magic & Mayhem

www.ingramcontent.com/pod-product-compliance
Lightning Source LLC
Chambersburg PA
CBHW020912310726
48980CB00011B/854/J

9780639844886